Also by the author and available
in English translation

The Twins

a bed in heaven

a bed in heaven

Tessa de Loo

Translated from the Dutch by
Ina Rilke

The financial support of the Foundation for the Production and
Translation of Dutch Literature is gratefully acknowledged.

Library of Congress Cataloging-in-Publication Data

Loo, Tessa de.
[Bed in de hemel. English]
A bed in heaven / Tessa de Loo ; translated from the Dutch
by Ina Rilke.
p. cm.
ISBN 1-56947-316-1 (alk. paper)
I. Rilke, Ina. II. Title.

PT5881.22.O524 B4313 2003
839.3'1364—dc21
2002030295

10   9   8   7   6 5   4   3   2   1

contents

Life tosses us up in the air like a pebble and
we say: 'Look, I'm moving.'

Fernando Pessoa

earth

Today I buried my father in Pest. When no one was looking I took some gravel from a nearby grave and dropped the little pebbles on the fresh earth. I stood there long enough to watch a yellow leaf flutter down from a chestnut tree and come to rest at the foot of the coffin. At the foot. Today, no yesterday, I buried my father. Now, in the Astoria Hotel at Kossuth Lajos utca number 19–21, I am lying in bed with his son. Does the fulfilment of a thirty-year-old wish qualify as happiness? Or can it ever be too late for happiness? The impossibility of our union has finally brought us together.

In the vague glimmer of the night my gaze slides over the furniture in reproduction Empire style, up the rumpled duvet, to the face of the man lying asleep beside me. He told me he has always loved me. I replied that I did not dare speak of love, but that my life has been incomplete without him, as if I had missed my destiny. Every experience I have had has been edged with incompleteness.

He will wake up in a while. He will get up, throw on his clothes, kiss me hurriedly and leave. Maybe having your wishes granted is the worst thing that can happen to you.

We needn't have met at all. Amid all those thousands of

fleeting encounters leading nowhere and vanishing without trace like evaporated condensation, this meeting was the exception. Did I know it right away? No, I did not. Yes, I did.

If I hadn't met him, there might have been more fulfilment in my life. More contentment, maybe, the kind of ordinary, comfortable contentment that I observe in other people. An absence of unhappiness. That may not sound like much, but still it gives people a sense of self-sufficiency. I often think of what would have happened if I had never met him. At times the idea of having my own separate self, untouched by him, is very appealing, and now and then I catch a glimpse of my un-lived, cheerful existence, like a negative of a never-developed photograph.

The law of cause and effect frightens me. A small cause and enormous effects. My grandmother sitting on a stone kitchen step in Buda, hearing a cello for the first time in her life.

Sometimes I feel very tired. Perhaps it's simply too much to keep dredging up all those events from the past. The effort it takes is forced, unnatural. It's the lives of others passing through mine, demanding, merciless. They turn everything upside down, there is not a single certainty capable of withstanding the onslaught of their tragedy. I need them as they are, as they were, the better to arm myself. Seeing the impotence of my parents in the face of harsh reality sapped me of all my strength, I hated them for their resignation.

Today I must make up my mind about a trifling matter: the wording of the inscription on his gravestone. But it is not a trifling matter, it will be a lasting memory, the proof of his existence. For whom? For a random passer by casting a casual eye on a grave.

Why, there lies Jenö Rószsavölgyi, 1915–1995, could he be a relation of the composer's?

heaven

My overriding memory is of a vast double bed. Outside, in the street below, all is quiet except for the occasional rush of a passing car. A car, at this late hour, a streak in the night.

I am lying on my left side, with my hand clasping the iron bar. I press my cheek against the cool metal. Sleeping on your left side is bad for the heart, my mother says.

From my position at the far side of the bed I look straight into the inky heavens. The night is both far and near. The mattress heaves like a raft on the ocean.

I'm eighteen years old, I have nothing against the night as such. But this night, while I am still in the middle of it, is one I wish to efface.

They try not to disturb me with what they are doing, they leave me alone. It's between the three of them. Perhaps my neutral presence there somehow makes it all right.

As I can't leave now, I might as well get some sleep. Running away would be childish, I'm eighteen and not supposed to be shocked by anything. Trying to force myself to sleep gives me a headache. In time, I tell the headache, this night will be utterly meaningless, even the memory of it will have vanished. Tomorrow morning, when we all go our separate ways, I'll be asking myself what sort of night this has been. And by then it will already be as if it is nothing to do with me.

I have yet to learn that it will last for ever, that it will keep coming back in myriad apparitions, as if this very bed, with me in my apparently superfluous role, holds the key to the rest of my life.

An outsize bed, suspended by black ribbons, rocking gently in the sky. An island where everything comes together and where everything begins. I can hear sobbing beside me. Stifled sobs, unsure whether or not they want to go unheard. It's not my friend sobbing. Diana is lying on the other side of the only male in the bed. The girl lying next to me is a friend of hers from college, whom I know vaguely. She is sobbing because of what is happening to her, because it is all her own doing. I could see it plainly, I was a witness. I believe it was important to all three of them for me to be a witness.

Go on, sob if you must, not that I feel any pity. I'm hard, I just hope you'll manage to sort out your life. I can already picture us all in the future, and even then I will not pity you.

It was she who asked us to come, me and my friend Diana de las Punctas. The student whose flat it is repeats her name with amusement when we arrive. De las Punctas, he mouths with exaggerated emphasis. Argentinian, Diana says, offering no further explanation. He thinks it's exotic. The name and the girl are both exotic to him, that is quite clear.

In a moment of shyness, the only shyness Diana reveals all evening, she draws his attention to me. This is Kata, she says, touching my shoulder. Kata Rózsavölgyi, her father's Hungarian, he'll play you a czardas on his cello if you ask him. The student's eyes shift from her to me. He sees me.

That moment, the moment when his eyes met mine, must have cut itself loose and floated up to a rarefied plane, from where – following a logic that is more earthbound than we ourselves, powered by some unconscionable wavelength – it has been undermining my will. It is an omen. A dragonfly feathering the water, taking flight, it is nothing, soon forgotten. It is all there is.

Was it Juliette Greco who introduced that dress? Black and waisted, with a little white pointed collar and white cuffs, like the uniform worn by girls at boarding school, but with a whiff of illicit longings in the dorm after lights-out. Or was it Brigitte Bardot who wore such a prim dress in the film where she smoked cigars?

Last season Diana had such a dress. When the fashion changed she gave it to me. The little collar and cuffs have lost their dazzling whiteness. On me the dress looks like a school uniform plain and simple, not a hint of untoward desires. My mother likes me in that dress, it must make me look virginal.

He sees me. With the uniform I'm wearing black flamenco shoes, just for the contrast. My mother isn't here to see. Of course he has already noticed my hair. I can't

very well hide it, although I usually wear it in a plait down
my back. People always see my hair first, then the rest of
me. The student also sees the milky pallor of my skin,
from which he can tell that I never get a tan, even if I
spend the whole of August lying in the sun.

I see him too.

The way he looks at me is different from the way he
looks at my friend and the other girl. There is a stillness
in his gaze, the desire dissipates, his mind runs the gamut
of reference points in an effort to place me. Some distant
reminder seems to be stirring in me too, as I return his
gaze. When meeting someone for the first time it takes
your brain a split second to register the specific configu-
ration of features, so that you cannot fail to recognize
the person for ever after, whatever the time and circumstances, even in the middle of a crowd. That split second
gives me a sense of recognition, although I have never
seen him before.

The moment has passed. The astonishment, the
incredulity, the subtle satisfaction that recognition gives,
be it nothing but a scent, a sound from the other side of
the world. The fleeting unsettling sensation vanishes
the moment he turns to the others, inviting us all to
come in.

An untidy room like any other student's room, a place
for study and sleep. Bed, kitchen stool, shabby armchair,
that is all his flat has to offer in the way of seating for an
evening that will last for ever. The student is not very well
mannered. He sinks into the armchair and crosses his

legs, leaving my friend and the other girl no choice but to sit on the bed. As if by claiming the only comfortable chair he is making them sit there on purpose, so he can lean back and make up his mind which of the two looks better on his bed – the one who has often, perhaps too often, lain there already, or the other one with the exotic name? I am to have the kitchen stool for the duration of the evening, on the sidelines.

Without a word, the student puts a bottle of wine on the table. He lights a few candles in Chianti bottles. A get-together without flickering candles, without fingers toying with molten wax, is unthinkable in the mid Sixties. The candles represent the dawning of a new age, and once it has arrived that will be the end of candles stuck in bottles. Long-play records are another stock-in-trade. The student rummages through his collection. You can see him deliberating. A Beatles album, maybe, to put us in mellow mood, or the Rolling Stones, as an assertion of his manhood? Carefully, lovingly, he places a record on the turntable. A waterfall of devotional sounds, unexpected in a situation like this, fills the space.

A Bach organ concerto. Heavenly harmonies, my father sighs, and shuts his eyes. His face softens.

He has to walk all the way from Sas utca to Szófia utca for his music lesson. A cap on his head, a cello on his back. He is eight years old. The sun dancing between the leaves in the trees scatters little pools of light all over him, and over the pavement too. He feels as if he were not making any headway. The tall houses on either side of Andrássy út cast deep shadows, the carved caryatids supporting the balconies seem about to collapse on top of him. The street where his teacher lives is falling away, receding, unattainable, menacing.

During the long walk to his lesson, twice a week, his aversion grows as he thinks of having to do the do re mi, mi re do, and then doing what his teacher, no his mother, expects of him: make music. He will hurt, the tips of the fingers on his left hand will go numb, he'll get tremors and cramps in his right hand from plying the bow. In the whole uncaring, immeasurable vastness of the universe there's no one more pitiable than the young musician grappling with knotted brains and a skull that feels it's about to burst.

Next will be the cane. At the slightest slip of a fingertip or an unsteady hand the cane will descend on him, harder than necessary, gratuitously. No need to spare the rod with him, his mother has instructed the teacher, he'll be grateful later.

Jenö is convinced the music teacher would have beaten him even if his mother had not given her approval. The cane is shiny from castigating generations of erring pupils. It is always ready and waiting for use, within easy reach. Jenö thinks his teacher wields it so rigorously because he can't abide dissonance, because, being so musical by nature, false notes drive him mad.

A cello is a heavy instrument when you're eight years old. The strap cuts into your shoulder. You wish you could be the street, the dappled sunlight, the shadows. You'd gladly change places with the poorest passer-by, who'd be too poor to afford a teacher. Anything to be absolved of music lessons.

Heavenly, love-thy-neighbour-as-thyself organ music fills the room. Diana and her friend sit stiffly on the bed like figures in an Edward Hopper painting, full of suppressed anticipation. They drink wine. The student offers them cigarettes. It's the first time I've seen her smoke. Nobody realizes how ridiculous it is to see her smoke. There is some small talk, but it soon peters out. The music takes over. The purpose of this evening with dripping candles and glasses of wine is not the sharing of ideas and experiences. Its purpose will depend on how subtly and surely the scenario takes it course. A wrong word, a wrong gesture, is enough for the actors to fall out of the roles they have cast for each other.

My role is to sit on the kitchen stool and act as if everything is perfectly normal. A tacit accomplice. As long as I can remember I have been trained in not-being-there, my parents are very good at that. I'm an expert in not-being-there, it has become second nature to me.

And yet, suddenly, all eyes are turned on me. The student has asked which courses I'm taking. My role extends to providing a brief interlude, a breathing-space.

When the music falls silent my friend and the other girl throw themselves into a keen competition for his favour, his desire. It's exhausting to watch, but there is little else for me to look at. Diana swings her right leg over her left, ignoring her miniskirt riding up her thigh. Her stiletto-heeled foot swings hypnotically. The other girl pouts, the way she has seen seductive starlets pout on screen. It's all been done before, nothing mysterious there, you think he knows where it's at, he'll think it's a laugh, after all, he's someone who likes Bach.

And he *is* amused. He lets it all happen, he is a superior participant without having to exert himself in any way. Merely to prolong the suspense he turns to me with a casual question.

The onlooker that I am responds dutifully. I'm reading art history, but what I'd really like to do is restoration, old paintings as well as modern ones, preferably the old ones, maybe. He raises his eyebrows. Why would modern art need restoration? Paintings can incur damage during storage in a damp vault, or they might suffer during transport, or be slashed in a museum by a knife-wielding madman. He nods, remembers having heard of such an incident. The silence that follows seems to be imploring me to carry on, not to stop now, and I go on to say that I want to study the traditional fresco techniques in Italy, and that in the meantime I do the occasional fresco on a friend's wall or ceiling, to get some practice.

Noticing that our glasses are empty, he refills them. Next he must do something about the silence.

Didn't you have a Bob Dylan album? Diana's friend asks. There's a hint of petulance there, of no more Bach please.

Conversation is made redundant by Dylan's plaintive, monotonous drawl, and for a while I consider slipping away. The trams are still running. But I'm glued to my seat. How much wine have I had, is he trying to get us drunk? An inexplicable resistance to the idea takes hold of me, pins me down. The possibility of simply taking off, and thereby saving my life from the direction it is inevitably taking, passes me by as surely as missing the last tram. At this all-important moment I am swept up by the sheer momentum of life, my will is a leaf in the breeze. For all my inaction, I am a party to their game, which is being played in earnest.

The first time I was struck by the invincible force of life was when I saw the photographs and the painting Uncle Miksa brought with him from Budapest after the 1956 uprising.

My father cannot deny that the eyes staring out of the photographs belong to his relatives, none of whom are still alive except for himself, a few distant cousins and his brother Miksa. Is that why Miksa brought us the albums? All the people in the photos look well off. Didn't the poor relations have their pictures taken? There isn't even a wedding portrait of that side of the family, just the picture of my grandmother as a girl, a watercolour painted by an artist with a taste for the picturesque.

Hey, you there, he must have said, how about posing for me? I'll pay you a day's wages, I'll buy all your garlic. She smiled, timidly at first and then mockingly, for whatever could he see in her? But she couldn't resist the temptation of a day off and relished being the centre of attention. Perhaps it was then that her legendary self-confidence was born. She raised her hands to tidy her plaits.

No no, don't do that, he cried, I want you as you are. Next she started taking off the garlands of garlic hanging round her neck, until he motioned her to stop. He wanted her with straggly hair and garlic necklace.

First I think she is looking at me, or rather that she was looking at the artist when he painted her. But I am mistaken, she is looking past his right ear. The pale grey eyes look past him, warily – no chance of running off without paying for your garlic. Like most redheads she has a fair complexion, and she is wearing a high-necked sandy-coloured dress, more like a pinafore than a dress. A child, still: ten, eleven years old. How brave she looks, and how innocent. You can't help being moved by the sight of her, even if you stopped believing in bravery and innocence long ago.

The family gather round when Uncle Miksa takes the picture out of his travelling bag and holds it up to the lamplight. We all stare, we share the same emotion. Uncle Miksa waves his free hand from the girl in the portrait to me and back again. He is agitated, his eyes glisten. Everyone nods in agreement: he's right. My father turns away, leafs through the albums. The portrait nestles in my mind's eye. A powerful image, untouched by the passage of time, just as Nefertiti is untouched by time. The image, once seen, can never be erased. From now on I am no longer just me, a contained self at the centre of the world as perceived by a child. I have come to realize that there is a 'before', that there will be an 'after', and I catch the first glimpse of my own mortality. I have discovered that I look just like someone else, and that the resemblance moved Uncle Miksa to wipe his cheek. She is inside me, everyone can tell.

I am the odd one out here. Once more the student interrupts the ritual of courtship to ask me a question. Would I fancy painting his ceiling for him, a picture of heaven, or hell for that matter, something for him to look at and dream about when he's lying in bed?

I know this is just posturing, that he doesn't really want a sky on his ceiling, that he's playing for time. All the same I nod in agreement, the cheap wine in my head makes me nod, what difference does it make – heaven or hell?

Uncle Miksa died in our house. It was a sickness of the soul, my mother says, but I know it was the sickness people die of when surgery is no longer an option. In the final days of the uprising, before the borders were sealed, Uncle Miksa packed up and left. When I shut my eyes he is there again, the first dead man I have known.

There he is, sitting in an armchair with a rug over his

knees. He beckons me to his side with the conspiratorial
air of Punch imparting a secret unbeknownst to Judy. He
crooks the same index finger to summon my father to
translate for him. My father is reluctant, he is not one for
reminiscing. Uncle Miksa begins with the birth of their
mother in 1893, that's as far back as his oral history goes.
She was born in a poverty-stricken village in Moravia, he
says, a hamlet really, just a huddle of wooden houses on
a muddy road, no synagogue. Sárika couldn't walk yet
when her parents left for Pest, where they moved into a
tenement at Dob utca in District VII. Her father set up a
modest trade in vegetables, fruit, seeds and nuts. Several
more children were born.

You give the door in the arched entrance a push, and at
the end of the passage you step into a rectangular courtyard with galleries on four levels all around and a tree in
the middle. The tree has longed so desperately for the sun
that it has grown disproportionately tall for its spindly
trunk.

Like Mother, my father mutters, she was larger than
life, too.

Uncle Miksa pretends not to hear. There are clothes
lines between the tree and the gallery railings, they're
always full of washing. The district is like a tiny
Jerusalem, full of Jewish families come from afar in search
of a brighter future in Pest. The courtyard is a hive of
smells and sounds, heated arguments, celebrations of
circumcision, the rasp of a hand-saw alternating with the
voice of a student intoning the Talmud, the smell of fresh
wood shavings mingling with cooking smells. This is

where she grew up, Uncle Miksa says, but just as the tree escaped the courtyard by growing sky-high, so our mother outgrew the little enclave in Pest, and she had no wish to be reminded of it.

My father growls in agreement.

Alas, Uncle Miksa sighs, she did not live to the age when one looks back on one's childhood with kindness.

My father won't live to that age, either, I reflect, however old he gets. So in his disaffection for the past he resembles his mother. I'm nine years old, but I will always remember what Uncle Miksa said. It won't be said again, I know that instinctively, this is the only time the past will be revealed. The strings of strange-sounding words reaching me in my father's translation describe a reality with which I have been connected since before I was born, although it has been kept from me until now.

Uncle Miksa thinks I have a right to know who my grandmother was.

I picture her in the bustle of the market on the embankment in Pest, or outside her father's stall at the Gozsdu udvar, which is not really a street, Uncle Miksa says, more like a corridor linking Király utca and Dob utca. There's a tailor, a bakery, a tavern, a shoemaker, a butcher selling kosher meat, a locksmith, a barber, a bookseller. *Fokhagyma!* she cries, pointing to her garlic necklace.

She goes round selling garlic after school. During the day she attends a Catholic girls' school, where she is taught in Hungarian. At home she speaks Yiddish. She has to go to school on the Sabbath, too, but on that day she is let off reading and writing, in keeping with the

compromise negotiated by the leaders of the Jewish community and the local Christian schools. To the envy of her
gentile classmates she just sits there, twiddling her
thumbs. Still, young as she is, she knows the saying *Z' is
schwer tzu sain e jid* – it's hard being a Jew. Which goes to
show, Uncle Miksa says, that her position was anything
but enviable.

The world my grandmother inhabited was just as real
as mine. Suddenly it occurs to me that people don't live
for ever, and that goes for me, too. I'm as likely to die as
the next person. Never again will I take things for
granted, never again will I look at ordinary, everyday
objects with indifference. Things can outlive us, just as
my grandmother's portrait, given to her by the artist
because it was just a quick sketch, has outlived her.

We must have respect for things, hold them in awe.
What about people? Respect or awe? I always have
trouble choosing between the two.

The last tram left long ago, so we'll stay the night.
Sharing the bed is no big thing for Diana and her friend,
as they've been sitting on it all evening already. Before
they slip between the sheets they take their clothes off
without a trace of shame, for that would be shamefully
middle-class. Having never shared a bed with anyone
before, I keep my underwear on.

At some point during this night I drift into a light, rest-
less sleep with the aftertaste of cheap red wine in my

mouth. An unreal, dreamed me is lying there now, reflecting that there are probably just as many ways of causing unhappiness as there are people. I am half awoken by someone clambering over me and throwing up in the wash basin. A vague nausea taints the remainder of my sleep.

After the night will come the brightness of morning with the illusion of a clean, fresh start. As if you could start each day of your life with a clean slate, as if, cleansed of your old self you'd become a new, clean self.

We pore over the leather-bound albums with gold lettering. How odd it is to see my own surname beneath a family portrait. It shows Yacov Rózsavölgyi with his wife Elza and their four children, Alice, Klára, Aron and Samuel. They look very grand, like the family of a tsar. They are prospering already, and will become rich in later life. Elza's beauty shimmers across time and the stiffness of her pose. Yacov, wearing a black beard, faces right, a faraway look in his eyes, as if he has weightier things on his mind than posing for a photograph. The children resemble each other – the cheeks, the round eyes, the small nose. Little white collars under faces staring directly into the lens.

There's a touch of voyeurism in our fascination. Could Yacov have imagined, when he posed for that portrait, that he and his family would end up exposed to the bleary regard of a grandson in Holland? As we turn the pages we see the children growing up, until in adulthood they are portrayed individually.

Aron develops into a self-possessed, sharp-looking young man, who seems confident of the future. Uncle Miksa talks about Purim, the Jewish carnival. *Purim darf man alles tun*, he chants, grinning. He has already discovered that I have no knowledge of the Jewish traditions. The name Purim, he explains, comes from the Babylonian word for 'fate'. Haman cast lots to decide when the massacre of the Jews in the Persian Empire was to take place. But the Jewish Queen Esther and her minister Mordecai outwitted him, and before Haman and his sons could carry out their plan they were strung up on the gallows. Purim is a feast, Uncle Miksa says, and everyone goes out into the street. Little children run around with rattles, loudly cursing Haman, the older ones wear fancy dress and masks. The streets are thronged with Esthers and Mordecais along with harlequins, cats, peasant girls, chimney sweeps and pirates. There is a ban on the drinking of water. Crowds seethe around the cafés, music and song fill the air, men wearing caftans dance along to the rhythm, humming the tune and swinging their sidelocks, until everyone is so drunk they collapse in a heap.

Aron, a pirate's mask and hair flying, jogs down Király utca with a group of friends. He hooks arms with a string of girls with gaily painted faces, and all together they troop to the nearest café.

Ad de-lo jadi, Uncle Miksa says, raising an imaginary glass to his lips, during Purim you must drink until you can't tell the difference between Hamann and Mordecai.

One of the girls, her face striped with red-and-white paint like a warrior chief, is Sárika Lajta. *Purim darf man alles tun, nach jontef stelt sach erois, wer e asponem war!* Anything goes during Purim, but afterwards we will see who has been up to mischief.

I soak up the past as a vivid reality in which none of us are of the slightest importance. A world unto itself. All those people dancing and singing in the fullest confidence that Purim will be celebrated, that it will be tolerated, for ever and ever. Compared with the bustle and vitality of the world conjured up by Uncle Miksa, my own world is padded with fluffy, fleecy clouds. You think you can lie back and dream, but you fall right through them.

Diana talks about nothing but him, the student, who now has a name: Stefan. Proudly, as though it were an achievement, her own achievement, she tells me he is taking a degree in physics, with philosophy as his subsidiary course. She tells me about his body and what it is capable of, reliving her ecstasy by going on and on about it. Her blissful drone gives me a feeling of envy, although I'm not sure what there is to envy. Diana's friend from college is miserable about being ditched, she says, which adds to her own sense of triumph and makes him even more desirable in her eyes. I can't stand to hear another word about her conquest. Has she no mercy? Falling in love has made her cruel.

Diana says he asked about the Hungarian girl who said she'd paint his ceiling, wanted to know when she was coming. I had quite forgotten what I'd promised under the influence of cheap wine. He really wants you to do it, she tells me, he'll pay you.

For the second time I accompany her to his flat. Again there is that strange, lingering moment during which we eye each other, that infinitesimal fissure in the expanse of time. In the pale light of day everything looks worn and shabby. Even Diana, who seems quite at home in the place, has a sallow, wilted look. The nights spent together are sapping her energy.

The idea of making a painting on the ceiling of this unassuming room is ridiculous. Heaven or hell, either will do, he'd said. But that was then, now he is adamant that it should be heaven, not with cupids or cherubs, no devils or evil spirits either. A heaven without Christian or mythological references of any kind, just a sky, actually, a firmament with clouds. Some sort of stillness into which his thoughts can vanish when he is lying in bed. As though his bed were in the sky instead of on the fifth floor of a desolate block of student flats. He will provide a stepladder, plastic sheeting for the furniture, paint and brushes. I'd rather buy the brushes myself, I tell him.

My wages are not going to be a problem. His mother will pay for the painting, it's her birthday present to him.

A week after Purim they are drinking coffee with cream and cinnamon at Café Herzl. They have not been brought together by a matchmaker, although the place is teeming with old *shidduchim* banking on a handsome fee from pious parents for a successful transaction.

Sárika's father is disappointed and hurt by his daughter's infatuation. From childhood she had been intended for the son of his friend, a humble plodder like himself at the Gozsdu udvar. Time-honoured friendships are in danger. Besides, this Aron Rózsavölgyi comes from a family of Reform Jews, who probably don't even know what the inside of a synagogue looks like. Aron's parents, too, express concern, for the sake of form, but they leave it up to their son to choose his wife, even if she turns out to be a penniless orthodox girl.

They marry in the synagogue, not in the orthodox one, although the Tabak temple in Dohány utca is not a bad alternative. On the day before the wedding Sárika makes a final concession to her parents. She takes the ritual bath to purify herself. The marriage, which is the wish of bride and groom alone, is attended by a large crowd. On the right are the men, on the left the women with friends and acquaintances. The bride wears a dress of cream-coloured silk, which will be stored in a chest in her bedroom for many years to come. Over the wedding dress she will wear an embroidered bolero, a Magyar fashion accessory. That mass of curly red hair piled up high, Uncle Miksa says, it was like a bonfire, a blazing fire blurred by the veil. His father told him so a thousand times.

For years his mother talks of the ceremony, the choir, the blessings (*I am of my love and my love is mine*), the giving of the ring, the breaking of the glass (*for our joy cannot be*

complete since the destruction of the Temple of Jerusalem). The
feast lasts until morning. There is dancing to the music of
the *klezmorim*, and all the men, from the rabbi to the poorest street vendor from the Gozsdu udvar, take their turn
to dance with the bride.

The things other people never achieve, however hard
they work all their lives, she was handed on a plate, my
father says. Thanks to her marriage she jumped up the
social ladder, skipping several rungs.

Uncle Miksa pretends not to hear my father's aside. Let
no one speak ill of the dead – that is Uncle Miksa all over
– no ill of the dead who were unready to die.

I spend every Saturday working on his ceiling. Stefan is
sprawled on his bed, smoking and watching the clouds
gather in his sky. The different kinds of music he puts on
engage oddly with the banks of cumulus flowing from my
brush. During Mahler they grow darker, more menacing,
whereas Bach draws my brush to the blue transparency
of the sky between the clouds. A cello concerto by
Boccherini inspires a tentative gleam of reflected sunlight, a hint of gentleness and warmth.

I tell him that my father manages to make this upbeat
concerto sound so sad as to make your heart sink. It's the
mournful vibrations of his soul that you can't help hearing. He utters little moans while playing, as if there's a
deep-seated pain gnawing at his cello, at his body. I think
the only way he can express himself is through his cello.

As soon as he puts his instrument away he retreats into silence. Sometimes, I say, grinning at Stefan over my paintbrush, having a father who can only talk to you through his cello is more than I can stand.

I shut up after that. I can't concentrate on the contours of cumulus overhead and talk about my father at the same time.

Well, at least you've got a father, Stefan's voice floats up to me. Mine died before I was born.

There is an edge of grievance to his tone, which makes me uneasy. My intuition tells me not to pursue the subject. I ask him airily if he'd like a bird in his sky, a bird winging from cloud to cloud. A dove, a stork, a raven, an eagle maybe?

Too symbolic, he says. Anything you would put in among the clouds, be it a dove, raven, stork or eagle, would be far too intrusive. It would push your thoughts in the wrong direction.

Wrong direction? I ask.

Well, if there were an eagle hovering in his sky he'd never sleep a wink again.

I stop painting and look down at him. What's wrong with eagles?

Kraut kid, he says. Those words would come to haunt me, I would think of them last thing at night, first thing in the morning, they would resonate in my dreams. Getting up and going out they would still be there, written on my forehead.

I'm finding it impossible to focus on my cloud. I sit down on the top of the ladder. How did your father die, I ask.

In a Russian prison camp, just after the war.

He is lying on his back puffing on a cigarette, nothing new there. His expression is blank, he could have been telling me about some film he has seen. From the moment I first set eyes on him I have felt there was something different about him. I am aware of the political and moral implications of what he has just said, I know what the received opinion is at the close of the twentieth century. And yet, none of that has anything to do with him lying flat on his back, or with me perching on the stepladder.

Did your mother love him? He blows out smoke. She says she did, the way people fell in love during the war. Emotions are more intense in war-time, she says, because death can come at any moment and ruin everything. Not that you lose sight of the distinction between friend and enemy, but there can be a shift in your personal values. But do go on painting, it was a long time ago, what does it matter?

A lot, apparently, I say, dipping my brush in the paint, since you won't let me paint an eagle on your ceiling.

He has made coffee. I sit on the ladder sipping from the mug he has handed up to me. He asks me whether having a father like that affected me, whether it messed up my life. To my surprise I find myself nodding. Although I have never thought about it in such crude terms, it is true that my father's gloomy silences made their mark on the atmosphere breathed by my mother and me.

He asks me whether I believe in freedom, whether I think it is possible to free oneself from one's destiny by sheer force of will.

My eyes widen. No one has ever asked me such a question before. Such a question thrown up in the air like a ball, which instead of dropping to earth stays up there, spinning round like mad so the dots on the ball turn into stripes. The longer you stare the more bewildered you become, you feel as though the ball is staring back at you, taunting you, challenging you. The arms you hold outstretched to catch it drop to your sides.

I wish I did, I say softly, doubtfully, I have the feeling things just happen to me. *Can I, can I,* my mother would echo when I wanted something very badly, no you can't but you may if you're good. I can't do what I want anymore than anyone else can.

That's a very fatalistic attitude, he bursts out, you shouldn't give up so quickly.

I shrug my shoulders. Wanting something and then actually going for it demands an inordinate amount of energy, I tell him, no one gave me any support.

Stefan sits on the edge of his bed, shaking his head. Newton, he says, who reduced everything that happens on earth to cause and effect, believed that things are therefore essentially predictable, and have been so since the beginning of time. That our will is not free. Schopenhauer went a step further. What we want is determined by our motivation, he claimed. When in doubt the strongest motivation wins. The strength of the motivation depends on individual characteristics and circumstances. Not very encouraging, is it? he grins.

I stare at him. Such thoughts have never entered my mind. There's an irresistible attraction about this way of seeing things, it feels if you can lift yourself up to survey the whole of existence. As if the spinning ball suddenly drops right into your cupped hands, making everything look straightforward and simple, deceptively simple.

Give me Sartre any day, he goes on, how about you, d'you like Sartre? I blush. Er, *Le mur* was one of my set texts, and I saw a play by him once, can't remember the name.

Sartre takes the opposite view: we're condemned to freedom, he says. We're intelligent and inventive by nature, we have the capacity to create and recreate ourselves. All we need is a conscious decision. Anyone idle or fatalistic will sink into nothingness: that's what he meant by *la nausée*. Such people die a living death.

I glanced at the candles in the Chianti bottles, which are still on the table. Are they the same candles, or fresh ones? Sartre is popular these days. Does that explain Stefan's enthusiasm? I wonder why doesn't he wear black all the time.

It wasn't until centuries later that Newton fell from his pedestal, he concludes. Quantum physics has shown that it's impossible to obtain sufficient knowledge of the here and now to warrant predictions. All we have is a probability curve. Certainty does not exist. But that's not all: the object of study is inevitably altered by the fact of being studied. Do you understand what this means? Mind over matter. How about that! Gets us pretty close to Sartre, doesn't it?

He gives me a satisfied grin.

I just nod, so as not to encourage him unduly. He's been dropping the names of Newton, Schopenhauer, Sartre as if they were friends he hangs out with, and I can't seem to come up with any suitable response.

If he were to fall out of his window on the fifth floor, where would that leave mind over matter? Could a conscious decision prevent him from crashing to his death?

I want to get on with my sky.

I'll have to think about it, I say, bending low to pass him the mug.

Pest stands for the plain, for progress and trade, for urban development. Buda is a steep bluff rising from the Danube, home to ancient Romans, seven Magyar tribes, the oldest Jewish tombstone (Rav Pesah, son of Rav Peter), and also the Turks and Habsburgs.

Uncle Miksa explains Budapest to us. Speaking of his native city from halfway across Europe makes him emotional, perhaps he senses that he will never see it again. It is in the hills of Buda that the rich build their houses. What more could you wish than a villa with a large garden in the wooded hills of Buda, where the air is pure?

Sárika has been sent to Buda with a delivery. It's a long walk all the way from the Gozsdu udvar carrying a sack full of fruit and vegetables on your back, she would tell her children later. She used to like telling this story, Uncle

Miksa says, she wanted them to know what happened to
her on that day in August.

She walks over the newly constructed Elizabeth Bridge
to Buda, climbs the steep incline and crosses the Tabán to
the residential neighbourhood on the far side of Castle
Hill. It is hot, Budapest is having a sweltering summer.
She is on her way to the home of a Jewish tobacco and
grain merchant. She will know the house by the carved
stone urns on the front, she has been told.

Rounding the corner she senses something stirring
within her body, a concentration of attention rising inside
her like a cobra to a snake-charmer's flute. A string of
sounds float towards her, music rising and falling as
though following the exact movement of a stroller in the
hills of Buda. What sort of instrument can it possible be,
where do those warm bass tones in the lowest register
come from, the altos in the higher one? It's a bit like the
gypsy *gordonka*, or the country *gardon*. Similar, but not the
same.

The music is coming from the garden of the house
where she is to make her delivery. Seated in the shade of
tall trees a gathering of smartly dressed people listen
attentively to a musician. A fiddler to her, she doesn't
know the difference yet. She is granted permission to sit
on the stone kitchen steps and listen. What sort of music
is it, she asks. The housekeeper kindly enquires on her
behalf: it's Bach's Second Suite for Cello. She memorizes
the name, so she will remember it as long as she lives:
Bach's Second Suite for Cello. She no longer feels tired
after her long journey, she is alight with the revelation

that there is music that can conjure up visions of infinity, like an everlasting balm for the soul.

She feels as though she has been asleep all her life and has just woken up with a jolt. As though she has had a vision of the different paths her life might follow, the assortment of lives she might lead, like shaking a money-bag so that the shiny coins scatter all over the place. She's thirteen years old, and discovers that she has a will. Sitting on the kitchen steps she discovers this potent force slumbering in the depths of her being, waiting to be summoned. On that summer's day, she will drum into her children when she despairs of their lack of willpower, I made three vows: I will play a cello myself one day, I will live in a house with urns on the front and a big shady garden where musicians will be invited to perform, and I will wear silken gowns edged with lace and hats with flowers and feathers.

There is no reason to believe she will be able to fulfil her ambitions. She is still living at Dob utca, in a squalid courtyard which always smells of damp, food and washing. She has come from the other side of the river carrying a sack of vegetables, her blouse sticks to her skin from the sweat. She has come here to discover that it is possible to create a separate world of one's own – after all, people on this side of the river have managed to do so. Yahweh can hardly think it's fair for people to spend all their lives holed up in damp, sunless rooms on one bank of the Danube while there are all those lucky folk on the other enjoying the most wonderful music.

Well, she got what she wanted, my father says.

Not quite, corrects Uncle Miksa, because they couldn't afford a cello, or music lessons for that matter, when she was the right age to learn.

She made up for that handsomely later on.

Uncle Miksa laughs, you ungrateful dog. He laughs, although he is the one who is going to die.

My father doesn't laugh, and he goes on living.

Stefan says it's time I took a step back from my painting to get a better view. He wants me to lie down next to him to check what it looks like from the bed. I take off my paint-splattered shirt. Wearing my T-shirt, I lie back on Diana's side of the mattress and survey the half-finished sky overhead. I notice a few things that can do with improvement. I can feel his hand. Everything in me comes to an immediate standstill. My blood stops flowing, my muscles knot, my breath sticks in my throat. My body and I will wait and see, take it as it comes, we're not even sure whether or not we want what's coming. The music has stopped, and I'm struck by how quiet it is under the canopy of his unfinished heaven. We exchange looks.

In his eyes I see the signs of trouble ahead, of tenderness, too, and other signs, but I'm just guessing. I feel his hand move. The hand moving across my stomach turns into the hands of all those other men that exist, known and unknown. The owner of the hand turns into someone else, a stranger I know nothing about. He touches my mouth. His finger slides up the bridge of my nose, touches my eyelids, my eyebrows. He wears an expression of incredulity, his lips are slightly parted, he seems completely absorbed in the scrutiny of my face. He pulls the elastic band out of my hair, undoes my plait. Now it's all those other men, known and unknown, loosening my hair with a sigh. Why do they sigh? Is it the colour they don't like? I am losing myself. This must be what it's like to make a parachute jump, to leap into space with your eyes shut and then float down, pillowed by the air all around, as though the very air were your accomplice and you a bird dreaming that it's human. But it does mean tumbling downwards from on high, down to earth, to life, to death.

Do it, I say. Am I saying this out loud, or is it just in my head? I want it. I want to fly in free fall, here, now, this is the moment in my life when everything tells me this is what I want.

But he draws his hand away and rolls over on his back. The moment has passed. Why Diana, why the other girl, why not me?

I must have relatives somewhere in Germany, he says – uncles, aunts, grandparents maybe, but where to start looking? And what if I track them down and get to know them? I dread the disappointment, imagine if they're super-German.

The tone of his voice is intimate. He is taking advantage of being so close to me to reflect on his chances of having a bunch of relatives in Germany. I couldn't care less about his German uncles and aunts, they are no concern of mine. The intimacy my nearness inspires is mine by rights.

Apparently oblivious to me lying by his side, all my pores atingle, he rambles on about his putative kinsmen. He has withdrawn his hand, the moment has passed.

It's hard to avoid becoming cynical, Uncle Miksa remarks, what with life giving us so much cause. Taking a dim view of everything and everyone seems such a convenient solution, but in the end a cynic is a man disappointed in himself. You must try as hard as you can not to become a cynic.

This advice is offered to me, but is really intended for his brother.

Blame garlic, Uncle Miksa chuckles, it was the garlic that made Mother so headstrong. Put too much garlic in a dish and it will taste of nothing else.

She ran the family like a general, my father says.

His brother makes soothing noises. All she wanted was for her dreams to come true, and she believed a strong will would do the trick. And she did get her house eventually, although not in the hills of Buda, but in Lipótváros. An elegant mansion with a balcony across the full width of the front and statues flanking the entrance, with large rooms in which to play music. They don't build houses like that any more, there aren't the craftsmen.

I wish Uncle Miksa were my father, I'm grateful to him for playing down her disciplinarian side in favour of her determination. The album also contains individual portraits. My grandmother wearing a string of pearls round her neck instead of a garlic necklace. She is still as pale as in the watercolour picture, but fuller, more self-aware. She wears a satisfied expression, self-satisfied perhaps, if you see her through my father's eyes. Doesn't it occur to her that things might go wrong? You wish you could give her some warning. A ceremonial portrait of my grandfather wearing a watch chain like a Christmas tree decoration, one hand tucked in the pocket of his waistcoat, the other resting on a lectern. My uncle remembers the photograph being taken on the occasion of his investiture as professor of history.

From then on he ignored us altogether, I can hear my father grumble. He never took his eyes off his books and left everything up to her, and eventually she turned into a bossy, interfering slave-driver. Nothing escaped her. And when he wasn't engrossed in his work he'd escape from the house to play chess at the Széchenyi Baths or the city park.

He was a scholar in the best sense, an astute historian. Uncle Miksa keeps defending the memory of his parents against his brother's bitterness.

Spineless, that's what he was. He never stood up to her.

Once my father breaks his habitual silence, he can say the most terrible things.

And he wasn't particularly astute either, he goes on. Those articles in which he attacked Theodor Herzl and his Zionist movement! We're Magyars first, he'd say, and Jewish second. For what does Jewishness signify? Nothing. Some of us come from Poland, others from Germany or Transylvania, but we're all Hungarian. This is our home now, we are Hungarian. If the Arrow Cross fascists hadn't taken exception to that, he'd still be alive. No, our astute father was not forward-looking. For all his status and scholarship, he managed to miss the point: history has a tendency to repeat itself.

I only understand half of what my father is saying. I have heard of the Arrow Cross, I know they killed my grandparents and my aunt, but I have never heard of Theodor Herzl.

He went to bed with her again, Diana tells me. Suddenly I remember her friend's name. Merie, with an e where you'd expect an a. Diana is smoking non-stop, my bedroom is wreathed in smoke. I take a cigarette from her pack and light up.

What are you doing? she protests, I thought you didn't smoke. I do now, I say, there's a first time for everything.

Another cloud-and-a-half and his sky will be finished, then he can stare at it as long as he likes. I will take the money and never show my face again. The prospect gives me a feeling of relief, and also a presentiment of loss. There is an unconscionable need in my body where he is concerned. Yet another tie to add to all the ties already binding me.

His eyes gleam beneath me while I fill in the last section of the sky. Why does he seem so utterly content? Because he can have both girls, as often as he likes, whenever he likes? And yet, if I were not me but someone else, I'd still have come down the ladder and lain next to him. If I were someone else I'd have sent my own hand out to explore. Forcing myself to concentrate on my work, I am seized with the breathtaking idea that you could be free if only you could stop being who you are. Just willing yourself to be someone else is not enough, there's some obstacle but I don't know what it is.

I'd been planning to put a sunbeam in among the clouds. But I've changed my mind, he doesn't deserve it. Skipping the sunbeam means it won't be too long before the work is done.

His voice wafts up to me from below. I, Kata, am falling in love. I have never been in love before. My brush falters for a moment, then recovers its composure to apply an even glaze of transparent grey with sure, fluid movements so as to avoid every hint of streakiness. The sounds of that night come back to me, and the motions too. I am imprisoned in a cocoon of impossibilities. Why should I care whom he fancies? I hate being drawn into his private emotions like this.

There is a knock on the door.

My mother, he says in a conspiratorial whisper. What shall I do? I ask. Just carry on, he signals, she's come to see my birthday present, I asked her to drop by.

I try to avoid thinking about fate, which can strike at any moment, propelling your life in a fatal direction. A sudden shake, a rearrangement of the general order of things in the guise of an innocent, day-to-day occurrence.

Does he believe in fate, I wonder.

Fate is terrifying, there's nothing you can do about it. Imagine you're going on a trip. You're on the point of leaving the house when a friend phones to say she's failed her exams. You take the time to listen to her and try to cheer her up, and so you miss your train. You take the next one, in which you happen to meet the love of your life, who goes on to make you miserable because he's an alcoholic who was beaten as a boy by his mother who was abused by her husband who . . . Fate is a tiny cause producing enormous effect.

I am up on the stepladder when fate enters the room. My fate, and that of my father and my mother. Fate steps in, looks up at the ceiling and gushes: how divine. Fate has ash-blonde curly hair and blue eyes that don't tell you a thing. She wears a mink coat – the anti-fur campaigns haven't started yet. She claps her hands together at the sight of such a pretty sky on her son's ceiling. The son strikes a reserved, indeed, a wary pose. With fate hovering so close, the son cannot help being apprehensive, for it is his fate, too.

It would be bad manners not to come down the stepladder. My fingers are smeared with paint, so I hold out my right wrist towards her. I'm Kata, I say, Kata Rózsavölgyi. She holds on to my wrist for a very long time, staring into my face. First the flurry of fate's arrival, now this long, awkward silence.

Why don't you take off your coat, the son says.

The mother recovers her voice. Your name, she says,

you have the same unpronounceable name. A hush descends.

Same as who? There's a flicker of impatience in the son's voice.

Same as my lodger during the war. My lodger, she says, as if she owned him. I have yet to discover that she is giving everything away with these two words.

My mother hid a Jew in her house, during the war, the son explains dully.

His name was Jenö, the mother says, and then that impossible surname. Her pupils narrow to pinpricks in her blue-eyed gaze as she casts back in time. Her eyes turn to ice. She is Andersen's Snow Queen, the one who froze Kai's heart.

My father's name is Jenö, too, I say.

He was a chess player first and foremost, Uncle Miksa says. A historian by profession, but his passion was chess. Three whole shelves in his library were taken up with opening gambits, middle strategies and end games.

So he always had an excuse, my father recalls. Time for the return game, he'd exclaim, half seriously half in jest, I must get my revenge on so and so. And off he'd go, leaving us in Mother's clutches.

Uncle Miksa explains his father to me, so as to untarnish the memory of him that his brother, my own father, would have me preserve. He played chess in the sunshine in the Városliget, or he'd watch others play and have to suppress the urge to comment. He'd make his opponents nervous by getting up and leaving the board when it was their move, and when they'd made up their minds at last he'd saunter back to the board, prop one buttock on a corner of the stone table, and make his move with a casual flourish. To him chess was good sport, a war of nerves.

Did he take you with him, seeing as you know all these details? Is my father jealous?

You weren't interested in chess, Uncle Miksa replies, and he is off again, swept along by the flood of images. As if he were a very old man living exclusively in the past, my uncle, who's only thirty-nine, sinks back into the memories of his youth. In winter they play chess in the swirling steam of the Széchenyi Baths, up to their waists in warm water from subterranean springs. Men of all ages, men with and without hair on their chests, some with slim hips, others with paunches, bald men and men with beards. The silent ballet of their gestures. A forefinger touching a cheek, a hand hovering indecisively over a queen, someone hitting his forehead in dismay at a disastrous move, another taking copious notes of the game. The curious stillness enveloping the chess players, the unfathomable structures and patterns taking shape in their brains. As if you could see the opportunities for winning moves suspended in the vapour around their heads, waiting to be seized.

It must be him, the mother decides, what has become of him? How am I, with my wrist in her vice-like grip, to explain what has become of my father? He plays the cello in the Brabant Orchestra. My voice falters. I'm not so sure I want to tell this complete stranger about my father's chronic gloom, his bitterness towards the world and the effect of his aggrieved silences on the family as a whole, about my mother who eats a lot, her sweet tooth, her ability to make up for his lack of interest by putting on weight?

He never talks about the war, or about being in hiding, I say. She lets go of my wrist. So you're his daughter, she says firmly. I feel naked under her cool, searching gaze, no longer at home in my own body, something is bound to be amiss, there is no escape from that indiscreet, hungry, censorious look.

Is her father . . .? It's taken Stefan a while to catch on. He is dumbfounded, glances from his mother to me and back again as if there were some connection between us. But there is no connection between her and me, unless you count an intuitive, mutual dislike.

So the ungrateful bastard who made off and never even sent a postcard in all these years is your father? The son does not mince words.

I never said that, the mother says soothingly.

You must have, where else would I have got the idea? He grins at me to soften his words, to ease the sudden gravity of the atmosphere.

Yes, he left the house when liberation came, the mother concedes, he left without a word, didn't say where he was going.

And she saved his life, the son adds laconically.

I, I'll ask him, I stammer. I'd rather bite off the tip of my tongue than ask my father about the war. For as long as I can remember the war is a taboo subject, except for the time when Uncle Miksa stayed in our house after the uprising.

The mother drinks her coffee in the armchair the son always reserves for himself. Fortunately I have his heaven to get on with. I concentrate on creating an illusion of movement in the clouds, for clouds are always in motion. The transparent, ethereal tints I am using are a fair expression of the way I feel. The history of everyone I know passes straight through me, without me having any part in it. How I wish I could be the kind of person whose presence is felt, someone who is heard, seen and wanted, someone with a say in what happens.

The sound of a plaintive, accusing cello fills the room. The son cannot be denied a sense of timing. There is not a more poignant moment thinkable for this melancholy composition. One of the few things my father ever told me about his past flashes across my mind: after the war I had to learn to play my cello all over again.

Halfway into the long-play record the mother gets up to go. Give my regards to your father, she calls up to me, tell him I thought about him a lot over the years.

What is the truth? The question looms when Uncle Miksa and my father contradict each other about the past.

Is Uncle Miksa flattering their boyhood, or is my father making it out to be worse than it actually was? If the two of them experienced the same reality in such different ways, where does that leave the truth? I long to know the truth.

For his eighth birthday my father is given a cello. He already has a child's fiddle, on which he has learnt the rudiments of music. Not that he ever expressed a wish for a violin, or a cello for that matter, it was his mother's idea. She chose him, her first-born, to become the musician she dreamed of as a little girl sitting on those kitchen steps in the hills of Buda, hearing a cello for the first time. And he is undeniably musical. His teacher, who lives near the Franz Liszt Academy of Music, works the boy hard once he has discovered his talent. Educational discipline in the Europe of old is harsh, verging on the sadistic. Every day, after school, he must practise indoors for two solid hours. His mother is his gaoler. On the other side of the wall he can hear the whoops of Miksa and his friends playing in the garden. You'll thank me for it one day.

And she was right, Uncle Miksa says, you made it your livelihood.

But I didn't become the outstanding musician she had in mind. I could have had a completely different profession.

You'd have had a much harder time getting out of Hungary if you hadn't been a musician. Music is international, music saved your life.

She wouldn't let me out of her sight, kept track of every single thing I did. I was not allowed out of the house, she forbade me to join in sports. Your hands, Jenö, what if something happened to your fingers.

You were her pet, my uncle chuckles, her pride, the apple of her eye.

I was her creation, her property. The air I breathed was hers.

We looked up to you. Verónika and I, we envied you for your special status in the family. You were destined for greatness. When you were studying at the Academy you were unassailable, in a world apart.

Ah yes, the Zeneakadémia, my father says with a sigh. Liszt looking down on you from his throne when you enter. A temple for the worship of music. Crossing the threshold into the great hall you find yourself surrounded by black marble walls and columns rimmed with gold, a sarcophagus for aspiring musicians. You mount the staircase to the first floor, where, between the two doors leading to the concert hall, there's a huge fresco with stylized male and female figures by a spring. The legend underneath reads: 'The seeker of meaning is a pilgrim to the fount of art.' In my mind I substitute the text: 'No dawdling in this temple.'

I am dazzled by my father's rush of words, for I have rarely seen him in talkative mood. Indeed, I will never hear him speak at such length again.

The building is still in use as a conservatoire, Uncle Miksa says.

She was never satisfied. Whenever I was assigned to play a solo during one of our performances, she would be sitting there in the front row, watching me with eagle eyes.

But she'd come home beaming, cries Uncle Miksa, she used to boast to family and friends. Her son, one of the few Jewish students to be accepted at the Academy of Music. It was not for nothing that he shared his surname with the famous Hungarian composer. Son of Sárika, my son, concert halls the world over await you!

I don't remember anything like that, my father says gruffly, all she said was: why do you pull silly faces when you're playing? Mouth agape, eyes shut, you look like a half-wit. Making it sound right is not enough, it's got to look right, too. She installed a full-length looking-glass in my room for me to correct my appearance while I practised.

She did it in your best interest, Uncle Miksa insists.

Who am I to believe? How can I be sure whether Sárika – she is inside me, everyone can tell – was an ambitious general or a loving mother? I believe what my father says because he is my father, because it is clearly painful for him to speak of his mother, even if she is dead and past laying any claim to him. I believe Uncle Miksa because he rises to my grandmother's defence, because the picture he paints of her is fond and filled with yearning, yearning for the woman she once was, from her garlic days to her death on the banks of the Danube.

I used to think there was only one truth, the kind of simple truth my mother demanded me to tell. A truth based on verifiable facts, rising above its earthbound reality to attain a metaphysical level of supreme morality. Truth as an instrument of peace, the ultimate arbiter of conflict.

But it seems there are as many sides to the truth as there are witnesses. If Verónika had not been killed on that riverside (or in the river, to save bullets, Uncle Miksa mutters darkly), she would no doubt have shed light on yet another side. Are there any conclusions I might draw from these conflicting truths? What would my grandmother herself have told me if she had ever met me? Am I the kind of person I think I am, or does it all depend on who is observing me?

Do give my regards to your father. For the next week her words reverberate in my head like the steady rumble of an approaching thunderstorm. I have a feeling my parents would not thank me for passing on her regards.

I try to coax my mother into telling me about my father's past, treading very carefully so as not to rouse any suspicions. I wonder why Dad never talked about the time he spent in hiding, I venture. Because he'd rather put all that behind him. Why? Because it was the worst time of his life. My mother glances at me defensively. What was so awful? I can see her hesitate. It's not a secret, is it? I don't think your father would want me to discuss it. But I'm his daughter, I persist, and anyway, it was ages ago.

She pours us coffee. Helps herself to a biscuit from the tin, then another. There is a curious correlation between what my mother puts in her mouth and what goes on inside her. It's a reflex action, a chronic hunger of the soul gnawing at the body, which in turn demands cosseting and soothing with a constant supply of food. She sighs. Her plump hand reaches for a third biscuit. I never actually met her, she begins. Your father and she had an affair. It started before the war.

The way she pronounces the word 'affair' you'd think she was referring to a fatal disease. It betrays her feelings about sex outside the sanctity of wedlock. It also betrays her feelings about her own marriage, which has had to forgo the romantic gloss of an affair.

During the war, when he needed somewhere to hide, it was quite obvious for him to move in with her. In secret, of course. She ran a shop that sold comestibles, which stayed open for most of the war despite the shortages.

What do you mean, comestibles?

Fancy goods. She lived over the shop. Apparently it was one of those typical Amsterdam-type flats with the living room at the front, then an alcove, and a bedroom at the back. The alcove, which was hardly more than a big cupboard, had been partitioned off. From the living room it looked like a normal wall with wood panelling. Whenever a raid threatened your father would remove one of the panels and slip into the alcove behind, after which he would lift the panel into place and secure it from the inside. There was even a peephole at the back – a knot in the wood that had fallen out – through which he could keep an eye on things.

How could he stand the strain? I ask.

It wouldn't have been so bad if that had been the worst of his ordeals. But after a while she started an affair with a German officer.

That word again, with it connotations of life-threatening disease mixed with the kind of romance that is the prerogative of others. It takes a while for the implications of what she is saying to sink in. My eyes widen, I stare at her like an imbecile, stammer: with a German?

Yes. She said it would protect your father. Her house was never searched during raids.

Did my father love her very much? I ask. My mother glances away with a glazed look in her eyes, thinking of her fruitless efforts to be the most important person in his life, to be someone she could never be. She has lost the hope of being more wanted than the other woman.

My mother sighs. Well, she was his first love, she says. He couldn't stand it. I think he'd rather have been discovered by the soldiers than suffer this torment to save his life. Then there was the incessant fear that the German officer would notice something when he paid her a visit. He had the feeling they could hear him breathe, could hear the sweat dripping from his skin. And he was also terrified that the man would call unexpectedly and would find him in the living room, although she said he had promised not to call without prior notice. He's German, she told him, they keep their word.

Yes, I say. Germans do keep their word.

The conversation with my mother is etched in my memory, word for word. I can see the unfulfilment of her marriage with my father, for whom marriage was a way out, a way of putting the past behind him, not for my own sake but as a peace offering for my mother, a compensation.

My father's blonde lover had curly hair, curls dancing a fierce, warlike jig. She did not come to any harm, she emerged triumphant, she has triumphed over us all, my father, my mother, and me.

Did she care for the German officer, I ask.

How should I know? The very thought irritates her. She doesn't want to know whether the woman cared for her German or not. As far as my mother is concerned the woman had no feelings at all.

When did he tell you all these things?

When we first met. He never mentioned the subject again. I thought I could help him get over it, help him adjust to normal life again. But something had snapped inside him, I don't know what, but it was something vital. Like a string breaking. How can you play a cello with a broken string? And afterwards he learned what had happened to his family, yes, that came on top of it all.

Oh, he's gone off with the gypsies, Mother would declare to whoever cared to listen, they've stolen him! As though you'd been kidnapped! She was inconsolable, furious. Father took your side. He's a young man now, just as well he's in Berlin, the capital of culture, time he got some experience, let him sow some wild oats. Did it have to be gypsy music, Mother wailed. Her darling boy, who was destined to perform in the world's great concert halls, playing vulgar gypsy music, goodness knows where, in restaurants, cafés, in the street. He'll be back, Father reassured her, you'll see. But you never came back, did you.

For all my nine-year-old ignorance, the veiled reproach in Uncle Miksa's voice does not escape me. In the name of those for whom it is too late to protest, he reproaches his brother for not coming home. Not coming home when it was still possible to do so. Not coming home to share a common fate.

My father is defensive. I met a piano player in Berlin, he says, who told me there was plenty of work for musicians in Holland. After the Kristallnacht, we left Berlin together.

My father's shoulders sag, he looks drained. I can't stand seeing him having to justify himself. Notions like 'no one saw it coming' have yet to enter my consciousness. My father's back is stooped. Did that come from carrying his cello up and down Andrássy út? From being beaten with the cane? From being forced to sit hunched over his instrument when his body was still growing? From his mother's ambition? From the reproach in Uncle Miksa's voice a moment ago?

I position myself behind my father and lay my hands on his shoulders. No one takes any notice of me. The atmosphere is leaden, until the pages of the album are riffled anew. The names of a string of cousins are spelled out, unfamiliar, inscrutable faces from another age, another country. All of them . . . all? Yes, all except one or two.

Suddenly all the different threads seem to come together in me. As if someone has turned a switch, making little light-bulbs go on all over the place. My father, my mother, Stefan, they know only part of what I see as the truth – my truth, which is true perhaps only because I wish it to be so. The way we make God exist just by thinking about Him. All the little pieces seem to fit, like a jigsaw puzzle. My newfound knowledge is a burden. I have a new responsibility and it frightens me.

Why not keep my mouth shut, put it out of my mind, all that stuff belongs in the past, in the days before I was even born, it doesn't concern me. But it belongs in the present, too, if only because it is there in my head, making it difficult to breathe. It's an explosive device, a landmine planted in the middle of our calmly resigned lives without there being anything I can do to prevent it from going off. My head feels heavy.

I can feel something inside me struggling to get out. Indistinct to start with, out of reach, but making its presence known with cunning and stealth like a throbbing, spreading ache. I ignore it. But it's like an onset of flu, you dismiss the symptoms until they come crashing down on you with redoubled force. In the ensuing fever I have a vision of two pairs of eyes gazing at me, two pairs of identical eyes with a sorrowful, defeated look that makes me long to do something, something crazy or good or kind, anything to banish the sadness, although I know it won't work. However crazy or good or kind a deed, it will not change anything.

Around the eyes two faces appear, ethereal shapes rising from the depths of my subconscious, where they must have been waiting all this time for the opportunity to reveal themselves in unison. Without knowing, I already knew. I knew from the moment the student opened his door to let us in. It started with the eyes. Then came the face, different and yet not different. The features less marked, less distinctive, but that's because he's young. There's much more hair, unruly, black and shiny, ever in need of cropping. My father's hair is thinner, streaked with grey and, of course, cut short.

A revolution takes place in my mind. There is nothing I can do but watch the ongoing struggle in silence, for positions of power are not easily surrendered. I lose my appetite, can't sleep, can't think of anything else. The delicate continuity of my life, in which my thoughts were free to go in any direction, has been brutally interrupted.

In any event, there is a truth of sorts here, an inescapable biological truth that is impossible to walk away from. The kind of truth that can throw your whole life into disarray but can also steer it in the direction in which it is meant to go.

I do not climb up his stepladder today. I have more pressing things on my mind than a painted heaven waiting for the finishing touches. Today it will transpire that his heaven has been a pretext.

Telling him what I know I notice a curious absence of emotion on my part. As though the story had nothing whatsoever to do with me. My voice sounds dull as I explain that my father was not just a Jew in hiding, but that he was his mother's friend and lover. The double cruelty of her relationship with the German. A two-faced monster, his mother, one face loving and protective, the other a mask of betrayal. The shocking abuse of the power she had over him.

He nods as though he knows what I'm talking about. His hands tremble as he pours wine, he downs two glasses in rapid succession. Does he really understand, does he realize what it all means? Did it ever occur to him that . . . Does he want me to spell it out?

As soon as I stop talking a wall of silence rises between us. I look up at my clouds, his clouds, but they do not ease my apprehension. I am unprotected, like Stefan, but right now he is more vulnerable than I. What am I inflicting on him with this new version of the seeds of his existence, why should I be the messenger? How can something that happened so long ago cast such a long shadow over the future, over him, over me? Surely each new life is entitled to innocent beginnings?

He gets up and paces the floor, clutching his third glass of wine. The wine rocks with every step. A hurricane whips the waves up to the rim of his glass, over the brim, the ship will sink, there will be no survivors. He laughs sarcastically. An eerie laugh rising up to the clouds. He paces the floor, laughs, shakes his head, sips his wine, wrestles with the altered self-image he must now fashion for himself. We all need an acceptable image of ourselves, one we can live with, which we can distil from the founding images we carry inside us of our father, mother, grandparents. For my own part I have exchanged my mother for the grandmother from Budapest whom I never knew. That helped.

Stefan has a confident, flamboyant mother, clearly accustomed to admiration for her looks, even now she is no longer young. But there is a certain acuity about his flamboyant mother, a serrated edge that can cut the skin. And now he has to substitute a non-father who was a curse despite his non-existence, by a new, real father – but what sort of founding image is there for him?

I've got to hear it from her own lips! he shouts. He grabs his coat from the peg and storms out without a backward glance, leaving me behind in triple anguish: for him, for myself, for my father.

Budapest is a beautiful, schizophrenic city. Two river banks that will never be united, no matter how many bridges cross the divide. The wooden bridge built by the Romans, the Turkish pontoon bridge, the Flying Bridge of the Viennese, the Chain Bridge constructed by Count Széchenyi in time for his father's funeral, the Elizabeth Bridge for which the medieval heart of Pest was demolished, the Franz Joseph Bridge with the Turul bird, the mythical father of Árpád who led the seven Magyar tribes to the Danube plain. So many bridges, and yet the division prevails.

You can tell at first glance. The mighty cliff of Buda rising steeply from the Danube, and the flat sprawl of Pest on the other side. Buda Castle on the hilltop competing with the Parliament building in Pest. Ancient and dignified Buda versus young and dynamic Pest. The waters of the Danube come from the Black Forest, passing Vienna on their way to lap the banks of Budapest, and then continuing eastward to mingle with the waters of the Black Sea. Water, such an elusive element: we hold it in or cupped hands, and it will trickle away between our fingers. Only extreme cold can bring it to a standstill, and only when the river freezes over does it truly belong to Budapest. In previous centuries the townsmen would take possession of the water in the form of ice by turning the frozen river into a fairground or a vast dance-floor. The custom came to an end in 1882 when the dance-floor collapsed under the weight of the whirling couples, who sank to their death *in der schönen blauen Donau.*

When the thaw sets in, the river speaks with a loud, cracking voice. Uncle Miksa once saw arms and legs drifting among the ice-floes.

In the mid-thirteenth century King Béla gave the Jews formal licence to settle on Castle Hill in Buda. They had probably been there already. Some say there were even Jews in the Roman army at the outpost of Aquincum, a little to the north of the town. Over the centuries the kings of Hungary benefited from the presence of the Jews, who assured a steady flow of money into their treasuries. There were times when the Jews fell into disrepute, as when they resisted attempts to convert them to the Christian faith or when the state funds were running low, and they would be forced to leave the country while their homes were seized by other people. But over the years the tide would turn and they would be welcome again. Welcome and needed. And they returned from far afield: Sarajevo, Belgrade, Sofia, Thessaloniki, Adrianopoulis, Constantinople.

They were needed, Uncle Miksa emphasizes, and not only for their contribution to the King's treasury. They lent citizens money at a low interest of 3 per cent. They supplied the town with cotton, felt and sewing thread, with timber and with cattle. They maintained relations with traders in Western Europe, the Ottoman Empire, the lower reaches of the Danube. They were useful in many sectors, besides offering credit. There was a brisk trade in exotic fruits from Asia Minor, Kilim carpets, velvet, muslin, linen, fine leathercraft from Morocco, contraband from Transylvania.

It wasn't until the end of the eighteenth century that they were allowed to live in Pest. They came from over-crowded Óbuda, from Bohemia, Moravia, Austria. They settled just outside the city walls, where Kíraly utca is today, and Terezváros. A Jewish market, a kosher butcher, kosher eateries, they had them all. His father's forbears, too, left Óbuda, grew rich in Pest with their tanneries and trade in furs. Later generations went to university, which is how my father came to be a scholar of history with a passion for chess. The family had long since moved away from the busy Jewish triangle to take up residence in the upperclass neighbourhood of Lipótváros behind the Parliament building.

Uncle Miksa glimpsed a hat, the sleeve of a coat, a shoe, among the ice floes.

I wish I knew how one is supposed to live. I wish somebody had taught me. Why do the people we take for authorities when we are children let us down in this respect? Who is to tell us which way is right? The cross, the crescent, the hammer and sickle, the smiling Buddha? Do as you would be done by. Are we hurting ourselves when we hurt our fellow man?

Stefan's mother thinks he's being oversensitive. He ought to understand that there was a reason for all the hurt, that it was all for the best.

We stare at the fleecy cumulo-nimbus clouds piling up like froth overhead. Configurations that speak of purity and innocence while in reality they are the bringers of cold fronts and hurricanes.

She did it because she loved my father. It was out of love for him that she slept with an officer of the occupying forces, the men who marched through the streets and searched people's homes. It was the surest way of keeping the search parties away, darling, surely you can see that? You must have some notion of what went on in those days?

So there is a possibility that he is not the son of the German after all. Yes, it is possible, probable even, considering the way he has turned out.

Why did she keep him in the dark? At this point the cold voice in which he has been questioning her rises to screaming pitch. All that abuse, all the name-calling he had to put up with on the way to school when he was a boy. The effort that had gone into picturing a father who was dead before he became a father. The constant longing to have a father like everyone else, the constant reminders that his longing was in vain. The struggle with his self-image, dented from the start. Why? Why keep it up over all those years while there was a real father? A real father instead of the phantom foisted on him by his mother. Why? For the first time in his life he sees his mother at a loss for words, his mother who is always in control, she is a bastion of control but her defences are crumbling under his salvo of why? why? why?

Because, because. Cornered now, she offers explanations. Because having a father who is dead struck her as preferable to having one who walked out on them, a father who didn't want anything to do with his own son.

What makes her so sure he didn't want anything to do with his son?

Because he suddenly turned against her once the war was over. He gritted his teeth, gathered his belongings and left in grim silence, without so much as a glance over his shoulder. As if she had been no more than a landlady all those years. How could she tell him she was pregnant when he treated her like that?

Then came the humiliations. In her neighbourhood, where many wealthy Jewish families had lived before the war, she had the doubtful honour of being the only local woman to have consorted with the enemy. That much he knew already. People sought vengeance, there were scores to be settled, and she became the scapegoat. They shaved off her blonde hair, they ostracized her and refused to buy goods in her shop. She has told him this before, too. There was nothing she could do in her own defence, for the only person who could have cleared her name and stopped all the hatred by simply coming forward and saying here I am, it is thanks to her that I'm still alive, the only person who could have done that had vanished without trace. No one had ever even glimpsed her Hungarian Jew.

I ought to have put some more blue in his sky. Why is there so much white and all that grey, what are those dark, heavy clouds doing over his bookcase, slate grey verging on black? It looks a bit too much like Giorgione's *Tempest*, if only I'd used more of the vibrant blue you find in Titian's *Bacchus and Ariadne*. He lays his hand on mine. We lie stiffly side by side on the bed like statues of a dead king and queen reclining on their medieval tomb, in thrall to the impossibility of love. What it means is we're related, he says dully.

Now the words have been spoken the realization comes crashing down inside me like a rock hitting a cold, hard floor. I feel abandoned, cut off from something that will never begin. I feel a great need for some kind of guidance, but don't know where to look for it.

We get up from the bed and cross to the wash basin, look at ourselves in the mirror, side by side. Above the shelf with shaving gear his head and mine, mine and his, reflected together. What we see is the past, the past where the laws of cause and effect are supposed to cancel out chance, and yet chance has had a lot to do with it, so much in fact that you wonder whether all this was meant to be, or whether things might have turned out in a completely different way. Of all the potential scenarios this is the one we find ourselves in, it is there in the mirror staring us in the face, and we regard it, dazed and bewildered. The way you turned out, she had said. He doesn't know this yet, but the faces in the mirror belong to my father and my grandmother. Our mothers have had no effect on the way we look. Coincidence or Mendel's law of heredity? We look in the mirror and see our ancestors. The ties binding him, binding me, beam back at us from his eyes, my eyes. From now on we have no choice but to look at the future through the eyes of the past.

He puts his arm around my shoulders. When can I meet him, he says.

Colours change under different light conditions, Uncle Miksa maintains. Colour is a matter of personal opinion. Some people claimed that the Danube ran red in the winter of 1944, others said it was brown.

Sárika and Aron have acquired a *Schutzpass* from the Vatican at considerable cost, for themselves and for Verónika, who has just turned fourteen. There are all sorts of passports nowadays, Red Cross ones as well as Swedish, Swiss, Spanish, Portuguese. Genuine ones and fake ones. Uncle Miksa explains how it worked. It's only twelve years ago, he can remember exactly. According to an agreement brokered by the embassies of the non-aligned states with the Arrow Cross, special houses were to be reserved in Budapest for Jews in possession of safe-conduct passes. In return for their generous concession the Fascist government hoped to gain official recognition from the countries involved. But the recognition did not come, and some of the houses lost their neutral status. One such address was Pozsonyi út number 30, which had been under the protection of the Vatican.

My father says it's all right for Uncle Miksa to tell me what happened. He thinks I'm old enough to know. And it's all true, none of it has been made up. Nobody in his right mind would, could ever make this up. The facts are established in a flat, almost disembodied voice, which is the only shield the speaker can put up against truths that can neither be faced nor grasped. Uncle Miksa fixes his eyes on some indeterminate point in the distance.

It is dark when the Arrow Cross raid the house. The occupants of number 30 who thought they were safe are rounded up and marched to the Danube at gunpoint. They are ordered to hand over any valuables they have with them, some of them are forced to undress, others are beaten.

The three of them stand there in our mind's eye, and we understand. Let it be quick, I hope. I try to picture my aunt Verónika, just a few years older than I am now, but I daren't. How can I have been so trustful all my life, there's no reason to have any trust at all.

The Danube is red, some say. The Danube is brown, say others. It depends on what time it is when you look at the river, and on what you wish to see. Uncle Miksa, owner of a Swedish passport and staying at one of Raoul Wallenberg's safe houses, went to the bank of the Danube and saw all sorts of things bobbing among the ice-floes.

I feel as if I've suddenly been asked to play God. Is it right for me to do this? I don't know whether it is right or wrong, but I simply must.

I ask my father to bring me the book case he promised me some time ago. The metal shelves in my room are overflowing, there are piles of books all over the place. It's time I got all my books into some sort of order, I tell him. This strikes a chord in my father, who is neat and orderly by nature. Besides, I have an interesting proposition for him. They're playing Bartók's Second String Quartet at the Concertgebouw next Sunday afternoon, why doesn't he come then and we could go there together. Whenever my father and I decide to go to a concert you can be sure my mother won't come along. Love and music have robbed her of him. She thinks she's too fat to be seen at concerts.

The die is cast. Stefan knows. I am a tenuous link between him and my father. I am afraid that it will turn out to be utterly devastating for one of them, if not both. I pray my father will be spared. I cannot protect him against the consequences of his own past.

From my rented room overlooking a narrow canal I can see the water being buffeted by the wind, churning and gurgling along the sides. A metallic gleam lies over the choppy surface. Standing by the window I reflect on the impossibility of breaking free. Going away and never coming back. Living out in the world, not in your family. Setting off on a dusty trail under antique lighting and disappearing over the horizon. Sitting on a river bank in the shade of a popular tree and staring at the reflection of the houses on the other side, fixed in a pose of summer idleness, in the dappled shades of Monet.

The swirling water in the canal reminds me of what has become of my freedom to follow my own inclinations: it has been washed away.

We listen to the cello in Bartók's Second String Quartet with the violins taking the lead. The opening movement has a faraway sound, as though it is coming from a place you had forgotten existed, a room in the depths of a large house. There is a strangeness to the moody composition that creeps up on me, filling me with a sense of desolation. My ears prick up at a sudden, startling pizzicato passage on the cello, almost like a drum roll. I steal a look at my father beside me. He is listening, eyes closed, letting the music pour into the most intimate regions of his soul. How well do I know my father? He is simply my father, a familiar stranger. But I can sense his vulnerability, and I am ashamed of what I am about to do to him. Will I regret it later? He will be dead and gone one day – will I regret it then?

My unease grows during the second movement. The hurried pace casts me headlong into the tumult of the world and the whims of fate. There's a peasant resonance there, a touch of the orient. A distant memory of the Magyars, the Ottomans? Glancing down at the programme on my lap I read that Bartók composed this piece during the First World War, in a village not far from Budapest. He followed the events with passionate interest, yet he never stopped composing. He himself was astonished at his ability to work under the circumstances, and wrote to his mother saying: it seems that modern warfare cannot silence the muses.

I am in no mood to sit still and listen to music. This concert is an offering to my father, made to propitiate him and lower his guard. The final movement, more cerebral by nature, comes as a relief. I am able to breathe again. The mood is one of introspection, of a conversation being conducted with oneself. The programme cites a Hungarian critic who likened the music to 'the profound interiorized nocturnal monologue of a lonely man.'

The end comes with two low notes plucked from the strings of the cello. Abrupt, dry pizzicatos, bold and at the same time mysterious. Then it is over.

My father sets about reassembling the bookcase, which has been taken apart for the journey. The inevitable must take its course. The time is drawing near. I hover around him anxiously, studying him from all angles, desperate for clues to his former, separate life which ended before I was born and which is still unaccounted for.

Stefan rings the doorbell at the appointed hour. Answering the door and finding him on the doorstep I am seized with the absurdity of this reversal of roles. Face to face again, although this time it is me opening the door and him waiting to be let in. After a cautious initial glance in my direction, he avoids meeting my eyes. He hesitates briefly on the threshold. I show him in and say this is Stefan, a friend. My father draws himself up and with a plank in one hand absentmindedly extends the other to my visitor. We drink coffee while my father returns to the bookcase. Stefan stammers an offer to help. He is visibly perturbed by this sudden encounter with a flesh-and-blood father, who politely declines assistance, saying the work is almost done. I marvel at how normal everything appears on the surface. Stefan keeps giving my father sidelong looks. He is at an advantage because he knows more than my father. There is a painful imbalance between them.

The bookcase-alibi is working, after a fashion. My father sits down at last. I bring him another cup of coffee. Drinking coffee together is reassuring, like passing round a peace pipe. Coffee mollifies adversaries and victims alike. I wonder which of the two my father is, adversary or victim.

Stefan and I, we have something to tell you.

That's a start. But what a start it is! There is a glint of alarm in the look my father gives Stefan and me: no doubt he thinks we're about to tell him we want to get engaged. His daughter being taken away from him by a total stranger, the first young man to cross her path – surely he's the victim.

Stefan's mother is Ida Flinck, Dad, he was born on 23 November 1945.

I speak rapidly and tonelessly, as if I have learnt the words by rote. And so I have, for I have said them over and over to myself before letting them loose on reality.

No need to spare the rod, my grandmother had told the music teacher. The look he must have worn then comes back to haunt his face: it hurts, but I'm not going to show it.

My father repeats the name carefully, checking whether it still fits in his mouth. After so many years. After everything that has happened. He casts a searching, guarded look at Stefan.

So she had a son, he says.

She *still* has a son, I correct him.

Stefan laughs nervously. I always thought my . . . I always thought it was Helmut Schwabing. He died in the war.

Is he dead? my father enquires gruffly.

I always assumed Helmut Schwabing was my father, Stefan stammers, but now . . . Kata, and my mother too, they think I look a lot like you.

At this moment Stefan strikes me as the more vulnerable of the two, now he is offering himself as a son.

My father is distraught, scans Stefan's face for signs of himself. He is familiar with his own face only as a reflection in his shaving mirror. A moment ago he was engrossed in assembling the parts of a bookcase, and now he is searching the features of a total stranger for points of resemblance with his mirror image. Is he recalling visions from the past, is he hearing the words people say to each other, in love and in fear? He is lonelier than ever. There is nothing I can do to help him.

Stefan stares at him in a trance. He is unaware of the havoc being created, oblivious to feelings of regret, shame, remorse, helplessness. He cannot conceive of my father's profound emotions. He is a witness to the birth of something new. He is the entranced witness to the birth of his father.

From one moment to the next my father, his father, is charged with an impossible task: to rearrange the order reigning in his mind, to come up with a fatherly reaction, to muster some measure of dignity in the eyes of his daughter and the young man who might or might not be his son.

He rises to his feet. Gropes wildly for his coat, as if that would solve everything. He tries hard to conceal his emotion, surveys his work on the bookcase which was nothing but a trick to get him here, glances uneasily around the room. He looks at me, then at Stefan. I think we had better – he clears his throat – take a little walk together. The invitation is addressed to Stefan, not me. Stefan jumps up and helps his newly acquired father into his coat.

I hear the door bang at the bottom of the stairs and watch them from the window as they stroll along the canal in the lamplight. Father and son. The result of a brief moment of pleasure that turned in upon itself. The very notion of pleasure in that context scares me. I can't help associating it with that barbaric stage of humanity during which pleasure was concomitant with violence, cruelty, indifference. It is easier for me to imagine life in the far reaches of the universe than to conceive of my father's passion. His passion for the woman with ice crystals in her eyes.

In August 1496 there was a pogrom on Castle Hill in Buda, which was described by Bonfini as follows: 'a riot in the street of the Jews caused by young, irresponsible Christians, who raised a hue and cry at the doors of the Jews and threw rocks through the windows. When the Jews tried to chase them away, they were set upon by a crowd of reprobates, mostly indigents seeking to destroy and plunder . . .'

Nothing has changed in four-and-a-half centuries. Uncle Miksa, armed with his safe Swedish passport, survived. Jenö returned to Budapest after the war, but did not stay long. The brothers fell into each other's arms and wept the way men weep, but soon found themselves shrinking from the unspeakable. There was no funeral to be organized, and no way they could give expression to their grief. Nothing is known of Jenö's wanderings in the scarred city of his youth, only the outcome. He did not wish to remain there because it would never be the same as before. He must have seen Castle Hill, laid waste as it had been several times before in past ages. He must have stood on the bank of the Danube, he must have wondered where the water he saw then was when it all happened.

Still at the source in the Black Forest? If you launch a toy boat on the stream there, how long will it take to reach Budapest? And how long before it reaches the Black Sea? How can a river that rises in a black forest and discharges in a black sea be celebrated as blue?

He is thinking of his father, the respected historian, for whom history represented an object of study, of interpretation, within the safety and seclusion of lecture halls and libraries. Is it possible that he failed to see that history is a panopticon of suffering? That the cardboard figures he pointed out and the names he juggled stood for people of flesh and blood? Now he himself has become part of the history of mankind, swept off the chessboard of the world. His sons will have to forgo his brilliant interpretation of these events.

Where's Stefan?

Gone home, my father mumbles.

Where did you go with him?

We went to a café round the corner.

That is all he will tell me. He avoids my eyes, collects his tools. He does not make the impression of a broken man. That reassures me. Kissing me goodbye he makes me promise not to say anything to my mother. Not ever. I try to gauge his mood but he is his usual tight-lipped, distant self. You can't get near my father, it's impossible to pin him down, to say this is my father, this is what he's like, tell him he has a twenty-year-old son he didn't know about and he'll burst into tears or laughter, he won't believe it. But there is no sign of emotion, I have to content myself with the conspiracy between him and me, a small token of trust.

After he has gone I start filling the bookcase. How should I sort them, I wonder, in alphabetical order or according to subject or genre? A mass of illustrated gallery guides, exhibition catalogues, histories of art, artist's handbooks, many of them bought for next to nothing in second-hand bookshops, finally standing upright in neat rows on proper bookshelves. One by one they pass through my hands. Early Renaissance in Italy (why am I being kept in the dark?), the Celtic-Germanic Style (why did they go off and leave me all alone?), Abstract Expressionism (my God what have I done?)

Gradually I come under the soothing spell of having to create order, a task which, for as long as it lasts, offers welcome relief from the complete lack of structure in my own life. Now and then I come across an art book I had forgotten about and flip through the pages with descriptions of tempera painting, the origins of oil paints, the pointillist technique.

My landlady calls me to the phone. It is my mother. Where's your father? It's ten o'clock, he should have been home ages ago. I don't know, he left at about six, perhaps he stopped for something to eat on the way home. But he never does that, my mother wails, he never goes to a restaurant on his own. Her panic sweeps over me. Long after my mother has hung up I am still standing there holding the receiver, as if replacing it would bring instant catastrophe.

The landlady pokes her head round the door. Hurry up will you, you're not the only one in this house to need the phone, she says, we're expecting a call ourselves.

I go up the stairs to my room, lift my winter coat from its peg, then hang it up again. I desperately want to ring Stefan and ask him how it went, but I don't dare use the phone again. I'm imprisoned within this house, within myself, within the irreversibility of what I have done. There are still a few books left lying on the floor. I pick one of them up, open it at random, suddenly convinced that the first illustration I see will have something to do with my predicament. I happen upon a reproduction of a painting from the Romantic period, the *Nightmare* by the Swiss artist Fuseli. A young woman wearing a thin nightdress lies asleep in an attitude of almost pathetic surrender. Crouching on top of her sits the devil, gloating and full of menace. There is also a spectral white horse's head with empty eyes like a marble statue looming over the sleeping, prey-like figure of the girl. Am I dreaming, are the devils and fabulous beasts only there in my head, phantasms of my own delirium? Will I wake up drenched in sweat, myself prey to an overwrought imagination?

I did what I had to do. I couldn't possibly have kept my discovery to myself, the truth was too big for my body to contain. It was not within my power to remain silent, so what is there to feel guilty about? Telling myself this doesn't help. The idea that I might have had no choice in the matter at all, that an extraneous force had dictated my action, is at least as terrifying as the possibility of guilt. Because where does that leave my freedom?

The phone rings. For you again, the landlady shouts.
Her voice is angry. It's your father this time, tell them not
to phone such a lot, will you.

I'm home, he says.

Uncle Miksa took a degree in engineering after the war. He
was involved in the reconstruction of Budapest's bridges,
all seven of them destroyed by the retreating German
army. As a boy he used to admire the bridges from the
embankment, or he would walk across them for the sheer
fun of it. He loves bridges, is intrigued by the mysterious
compromise between soundness of construction and ele-
gance. The seven bridges link Pest with the south. Bridges
symbolize peace and human contact, which is why the
Germans blew them all up. To Uncle Miksa, a keen chess-
player like his father before him, building a bridge is like
making a strategic, winning move on the chessboard. A
beautiful bridge is a poem, he says. He dreams of being
chosen to design the eighth bridge. It will be sheer poetry.

But in the autumn of 1956, at the time of the uprising,
he is already stricken with the disease that will eventually
kill him. Nevertheless he joins the march to the statue of
freedom fighter Jószef Bem. He is there when Imre Nagy
addresses the crowd, he is there when the Russian tanks
roll into Budapest. But he isn't there any more when
Nagy is executed.

Just before the borders are closed he leaves Hungary to
visit his brother in Holland, in a last, half-hearted attempt

to find a cure for his disease. In his leather travelling bag he brings the photo albums and the portrait, which his mother gave to non-Jewish friends for safe-keeping before seeking refuge in the quarters reserved for Jews with Vatican documents. He entrusts them to the last surviving members of the family to whom the people in the photographs are not strangers. Which is as it should be, given that the purpose of all those photographs was to show future generations who their forbears were, to tell them: without us you would not have existed, this is what we looked like, how we lived, thought, felt, hoped and made plans, just like you. We lived. Memento vivere. The time will come for you, too, when all there is left of you is a painted portrait or some photographs in an album. When there is no one left to recognize us in the pictures, we die a second death.

His sky is finished. Stefan is lying by my side, gazing up at the clouds dreamily, contentedly. It is a serene sky, indeed heavenly, and it creates a false sense of security. Personally I would have preferred to have a demon and the spectre of a white horse among the clouds.

We lie side by side without speaking. I can feel the heat of his body, and yet there is a numbing chill, the chilling realization that he is out of my reach for ever. The desire felt by the person I was before his mother came to inspect his heaven – and gave fate a jolt in the process – is still there. Like hay in spontaneous combustion.

Lying next to him is blissful torture, so close and so apart. I do not recognize myself in the girl beside him, have not yet discovered the mechanisms of my body, my body which shares half his genes.

I don't know whether to laugh or cry, he says.

What does he mean? I don't want to know. I wish time would stand still right now, with us lying here together, before things are said.

So now I've found a father and lost a lover. The words are addressed to heaven, and they sound like an indictment.

Had I been thinking straight they would have sounded pathetic. But I am not thinking straight, for I have a mind for abandon to the most turbulent pathos, the most scorching passion, the most wrenching sorrow.

He gives me a stern, searching look. You must have realized that yourself, he whispers.

Hearing him speak makes me realize the magnitude of this cruel stroke of fate, which joined us together only to put us asunder. How powerless we are against the law of cause and effect, against other people's actions and the meanings assigned to them by others.

We look at each other, closer than ever, and the moment when we first met comes rushing back, him and me face to face in the doorway to his flat, eyes fastened on each other, the pang of knowing without knowing, the autumn light outside, the huge bed inside.

He kisses me gently on my face, his head hovering over mine. He unties my plait, takes my hair in his hands, brushes it with his cheek. His lips explore further, pass from my face to my neck to my breast. I long to do the same with him, but I can't see how I can be passive and active at the same time. It is not easy for me to remain passive, for I have yet to learn how to convert my own desire into the bliss of being loved. My motionless body tenses to his touch. He undresses me, kisses my stomach. I feel his hair brushing against my skin, and my impatience grows. I want him, here, now, I want the bed to creak the way it did with Diana and Merie.

He strips off his clothes and drops them next to the bed. I can hear them falling, the buckle of his belt clanking on the floorboards. I don't dare look at him, so I fix my eyes on the clouds instead. Time for the trumpets and bugles to sound in my heaven, I think, and I feel a surge of reckless defiance, I'll do anything to please him, anything.

I can't, he says hoarsely. His head sinks on to my chest.

I lift my hand in search of his face. It is wet between his cheek and my breast. I stroke his hair. If only I could bring myself to take action, but his words have thrown up a barrier between us.

My body begins to tremble, I can't stop shaking. I am cold, pull up the blanket to cover us. I've always known I don't deserve anything good, although I don't know why that should be so. What other people get served on a plate, what other people don't even know how to appreciate, will never be mine.

He rolls off me, shakes his fist at our heaven. Damn, he cries, damn.

Outside, traffic. Outside, the world. That which was joined in heaven has been put asunder by the world.

bed

My father is to be buried in the Jewish cemetery in Pest.

We pay a visit to the rabbi, who runs a small restaurant serving kosher meals. He says that since my father's grandparents (the lovely Elza and her black-bearded Yacov) are buried there, my father can be buried there too. Because those who shared the same bed in life, the rabbi explains, may share the same grave in death. Indeed, that rule is loosely interpreted, for besides husbands and wives it also extends to parents and children, even grandfathers and grandsons. He himself will, one day, be laid to rest in the grave of his grandfather, who came from Tarnopol in Galicia and who sold buttons and other sewing necessities at Teleki László tér market. The Jewish rules for the interment of the dead are not very different from the Hungarian tradition, by which a Hungarian not only never loses his citizenship whatever country he lives in, but also retains the right to be buried in the homeland – even his children and grandchildren retain that right.

That offers some interesting perspectives for us, too, Stefan grins. His remark troubles me. Of the two of us surely I'm the only one ever to have shared my father's bed, even if it's only a faint memory of early childhood.

We have taken two adjoining rooms in the Astoria Hotel, which is round the corner from the Tabak temple where my grandparents were married (like a bonfire, all that red hair). We are about to bury their eldest son. Now that I am here, in the old Jewish quarter of Pest, I am anxious to see the tenement house on Dob utca (in that courtyard filled with pungent smells and sounds, like a little Jerusalem). Before my father escapes me for good I want to bring him and his mother back one last time. I want to know what the images were that my father blotted out so successfully that he was obliged to make a pilgrimage to Budapest in his old age, in a belated effort to retrieve them.

Passing through the stone archway with heavy wooden doors we find ourselves in the courtyard. They came from a village in the backwoods of Moravia, I say, it's not even on the map. I tell Stefan everything I can remember about them. He nods eagerly, listens with careful concentration to my account of his ancestry as though in a final tribute to his father. My father never discussed these things with him. Uncle Miksa said there was just the one tree growing in the courtyard, but now there are two. Could he have been mistaken? Or has the old tree been replaced by two new ones? The façades are a dingy yellow, the wooden window frames split and weathered under the peeling brown paint. My eyes run along the galleries on all four sides. I know they lived on the first floor, but where? I wish I could summon her from the past, make her appear before us. If the material world has the capacity to conserve memories of people and events, then these façades, galleries, windows and doors must still contain within them the image of her until the day of her marriage. But the architecture is not forthcoming, it keeps silent, uncaring as to who once lived there. The past does not reveal itself to us, we are excluded, pushed forward to safer times. On top of a broken-down chest a white cat arches its back, eyeing us balefully. I cross towards it, reach out my hand, lure it with sounds I reserve for cats, but its back arches even higher. It is rigid with suspicion, ready to make a dash for it.

If only they had been a bit more suspicious.

You needn't bother to go there, the rabbi had said, there's nothing left of the old Gozsdu udvar. It's not even marked on that city map you have there. Still, he explained where we could find it, a sort of passage linking Dob utca and Király utca. We go past it three times before noticing the ornate wrought-iron gate marking the entrance. A wide, dimly lit passage leads to a rectangular courtyard with a sign on one of the walls saying *Epület* I. That means building number 1, Stefan says, after consulting his pocket dictionary. On either side the double doors and windows, some of which have blinds, recall the shops that flourished here in better days. Elaborate Art Nouveau ornaments suggest that it was once a smart, modern shopping arcade. Now it is deserted, except for an emaciated dog squatting to do its business in a corner. The entrance to *Epület* II is flanked by stone balls the size of watermelons. This is where her father sold his vegetables. Garlic. This is where she must have stood, shouting *Fokhagyma!* – I remember the word clearly – without an inkling that she

would ever have a granddaughter who would come looking for her ninety years later.

Epület III, *Epület* IV, *Epület* V. I'm standing in the middle
of *Epület* V. Stretching away on either side of me I see a
series of identical passageways and courtyards, dwindling
in size like the visual echo of a rectangle. I twist my head
from side to side until I'm dizzy. I have the feeling I have
seen this before. In a dream? The endless repetition, what
does it remind me of?

Come on, Stefan says.

The house in Lipótváros still looks exactly the same as
Uncle Miksa described it to me (they don't build houses
like that any more, there aren't the craftsmen). Their
apartment comprised the whole of the curved balcony
with French windows for the master bedroom, and
another balcony, six arched windows wide, for the dining
and sitting rooms. Between the two is the window of my
father's room, from where he could hear his brother and
their friends playing outside while he practised (you were
destined for greatness). We walk down his street. Stately
nineteenth-century houses, some of them richly decorated on the front. Drawing level with the Parliament
building we reach the Danube, where the rush of traffic
totally erases the history of the riverbank. For the
pedestrian there's a narrow strip of green along the
water's edge. It is late afternoon, the sinking sun casts an
antique glow over the buildings fronting the river. But the
water in the river is dark. What colour is it? Hard to tell.
Dark.

We walk in the direction of the Chain Bridge. Wait, I say, let's stop here for a moment. Stefan nods. He knows why. We stand on the bank staring out over the river. I know all sorts of things about that night and yet I know nothing. The water of the Danube is dark, unfathomable. Across the river looms Castle Hill with its towers thrusting into the sky like bastions of religious and secular power. This was the last thing they saw. Or was Castle Hill invisible on that night? Were they capable of perceiving anything at all, apart from their petrified incredulity in the face of the outrage?

Putting my arm through Stefan's I say it seems to me that the survivors were incapable of grieving properly. Because it was too awful, too incomprehensible. That they pass on this incapacity to the following generations. Perhaps it would be a good thing if they created a fitting ritual of their own. So as to get a chance to grieve at last, and thus to break the chain.

Stefan says nothing. This problem has arisen too late in his life for it to affect him. The only sorrow he feels is for the death of his father.

There's Count Széchenyi's bridge. All my life I have struggled to build bridges between me and my father. He wouldn't let anyone love him, but in Stefan I can love him anyway.

We drink Tokay wine from flute-glasses. All around us rises the bourgeois chic of pink marble columns and large mirrors, of gilt borders and chandeliers of Venetian glass. The place is full of old ladies. One glass after another is placed on the table in front of me, leaving the liquid gold to take care of conciliation with death and likewise with life. We move to the adjoining restaurant and order chicken with a stuffing of nuts and raisins. And some more of this wine. He says I'm beautiful, that I look as if I belong here.

You too, I say, and we clink our glasses and smile. Is this my brother? Yes, he resembles my father the way he was when I was eighteen years old.

They were on friendly terms during all those years. The music helped. They would go to concerts together or they would listen to records in Stefan's apartment and compare recent releases with older versions of the same music. Stefan showed no inclination to shoulder any vicarious guilt: as a son he was unblemished by the past. We managed to keep all this from my mother until her death. It would have destroyed her, my father said, and I think he was right.

Was I jealous? My father used to have an overbearing presence in spite of his absence of mind. Inside the ring of silence he surrounded himself with he seemed to be pleading for the very affection that he rejected. That left me pretty much empty-handed. I'd have stood on my head if it had made any difference, I'd have done anything to get through to him, like in the fairytale about the princess who didn't know how to smile. But he didn't even want me to sit on his knee. I found this hurtful, and I could sense my mother's suffering. Day after day he would drift off, as if we weren't worth his notice. Any tenderness he could muster was reserved for his confounded

cello. I'd rather have had a father who hit me, like Diana's.

He was there for his son, though, in a way. Why wasn't he there for me? Because I was just a daughter? Because I reminded him too much of his mother? Because he had been in thrall to a woman twice already? If it had made any difference I'd have stood on my head.

This is a very beautiful city, Stefan says, I can't imagine what made him want to leave. How could he hate his mother for forcing him to study the cello while he, as I knew him, was unable to live without music?

I'm sure he would have made up with her in the end, I say, but that love affair, and then the war, stopped that from happening.

And what a love affair, what a woman! He laughs, there's a hint of scorn in his voice.

The woman indeed. Thinking of her now throws us off track, the words catch in my throat. I take another sip of my Tokay, and yet another, and let the wine slide down slowly.

It is long since I last heard him play, but I can still make out his plaintive andante. The sound seems to come from a place where only the spirit of music is made, an unhurried, sonorous caressing of my raw nerves. All the things I don't want to know resonate in that sound, other people's secrets which are no concern of mine, the vaporized passions of those who are no longer with us, sandstorms unrolling a carpet of oblivion. I listen to the play of dead fingers, I register the utter pointlessness of an andante without an audience to hear it, an andante that will disperse at the first ray of sunshine. I sit bolt upright, drenched in sweat, blinking against the beam of sunlight shooting at me through the slit in the curtains. My temples throb with a searing headache, my mouth is as parched as the desert. Not very dignified, all this boozing just before a funeral.

In the bathroom I gulp down three glasses of water. It has a slightly odd taste. Would it be from the Danube?

I can image his heart sinking at all this pomp and grandeur, I tell him, he must have been scared he couldn't live up to such high expectations.

We wander about the Music Academy, founded by Liszt and guarded against diligence lacking in talent and talent lacking in diligence by his stern-looking statue over the entrance. The interior is designed in a lavish, exuberant style, which is referred to in my travel-book as 'baroque Art Nouveau'. The sides of the main hall as well as the octagonal pillars are of black veined marble rimmed with gold. As we climb the forbidding staircase I can feel the weight of a cello on my back. The first floor is decorated with pinkish-brown veined marble combined with blue-green tiles and gold, more gold. There are two entrances to the auditorium, which is equipped with a huge concert organ. This is where he must have sat, snuffling and pulling faces under the disapproving looks of his mother. Between the two entrances there is a fresco showing men and women in Grecian robes gathered by a spring. I had forgotten the motto, but there it is: 'The seeker of meaning is a pilgrim to the fount of art.'

This temple of music, in which dawdling was anathema, was completed in the year 1907, eight years before my father was born. I am beginning to understand a little of his mother's aspirations. Imagine achieving glory in music, when the nation's ambition was to rival Vienna! My grandmother was a child of her time.

We follow in his footsteps as he trudges down Andrássy út on his way home. The trees cast their tall shadows over him. He walks past the opera, another stronghold of musical conspiracy. Being forced to achieve the highest goals has undoubtedly had a numbing effect on his ingenuity and initiative. The wings of his imagination have been clipped, and it is only at moments when he is able to forget himself that he can dream of taking to the air and flying away. There is nothing more killing than having to strive for perfection. It eats away at him from the inside, until he no longer knows who he is, who he might have been. Deep inside him rebellion stirs, unbeknownst to him.

On the eve of the funeral we drink mineral water at dinner. Out of respect for what is to come or remorse over last night, perhaps a bit of both, we order some *kristály víz* instead of Tokay. We linger in the café for a long time afterwards, indecisive, carefully sidestepping any thoughts of the night ahead. I wonder if Count István Széchenyi got any sleep on the night before his father's funeral. I think of my mother's death five years ago, as a consequence of 'an embolism in the artery resulting from arteriosclerosis'. Using the clinical terms to describe that fatal moment when her heart stopped beating is to conceal the true cause. I try thinking about what is unthinkable, about the failure of the living to comprehend.

I'm going to miss him, I say.

He smiles, says I'm an orphan now. That I'll be able to cast off the burden of the past, get rid of all those tons of sadness that never did anyone any good. I can't imagine what can have prompted him to say such a heartless thing, on this day of all days, and I ask him coldly what he means. There's no one left to take the blame now, he says, from now on you'll have to take full responsibility for your own wellbeing. All that guilt in our family, it's like a boomerang, it keeps coming back to hit you each time you throw it away. And it wouldn't surprise me if you yourself were the worst of the lot, he says, since you've taken the fate of your entire family on board. He tells me this straight to my face without batting an eyelid. He's giving me a lecture like a brother, like someone who is so close to you that he's entitled to speak the most intimate truths. And how much do I really know about what goes on under that great load of guilt?

I stare at him and shake my head, unable to speak. Why is he attacking me? What I need is consolation, an elder brother's arm round my shoulders so that I don't break down and cry.

Rage, he maintains, rage is what's stopping you from getting a life, a proper life of your own.

He leans forward on his elbows and gives me an ironic

state. D'you know what sort of ritual you could do with? he asks.

No I do not, I say, seething with indignation.

A ritual that would rid you of all that repressed rage!

I look at him, stunned. Who does he think he is? He didn't even enter my father's life until he was twenty-one. How dare he pass judgement on me like this? Turning my face to the window I stammer something about psychobabble, that's all it is. I stare out of the window at the darkness of the city that is not truly dark. I'm on the brink of tears, but I'm determined he will not see my cry.

You're beautiful when you're angry, he says, clasping my hand.

I swallow. That's disgusting, what a disgusting cliché, I mutter, you sound like an airport novel. But as I speak my indignation dissipates, vanishes under his touch. It is his hand lying on mine, his living hand on my living hand. I start laughing. Tears run down my cheeks. He strokes my hand, suddenly looking very earnest. I ask him what on earth makes him see our family in these terms. Surely there are countless other ways of interpreting how the members of my family have related to each other?

The possibilities are endless, he says with a sigh, but there's no point in getting bogged down in speculation. You have facts on the one hand, and emotions on the other. Despite all the philosophical effort that has gone into undermining the existence of facts, they still warrant acceptance, if only in the sense that they're the illegitimate offspring of truth and, as such, instrumental in providing clarity. Our justice system, too, along with the code of law, revolves around factual evidence simply because there's no alternative.

This isn't a seminar, you know, I say with a groan.

He's not making things more complicated than necessary, he says, I mustn't think that, what he's doing is simplifying them. He taught himself from a young age to separate facts from feelings. His mother slept with a German at a time when that was considered reprehensible. That is fact. And he was the result of their affair – another fact, even though it did not last. The way the neighbours and his classmates at school, even some of his teachers, responded to these facts belongs to the category of feelings. A miasma of sentiments within a specific historical, political and moral context, which had nothing whatsoever to do with him personally. Seeing things that way had been his only hope of survival. It wasn't his fault, he kept telling himself, none of it had anything to do with who he actually was.

But the facts, I protest, what about them?

You're thinking of what feelings do with facts, he says, but a fact *per se* is neutral. Facts exist outside the world of our emotions, where we can't touch them or change them.

What a typically male attitude you're taking, I say to myself, treating the mind and the emotions as completely different things. In an attempt to hide my confusion I make a little joke about the spirit of Enlightenment breaking through the obscurity of the Middle Ages. I feel as if I'm on quicksand. His argument sounds reasonable enough, so why the deep-down need to put up all his resistance? Sharing guilt may well be another way of showing compassion, I venture. Maybe so, he says, it's just human nature and all that, which is fine so long as you don't drown in it. His mouth curves up at the corners. He strokes my cheek. As for that family of yours, he says, I can assure you that I know the facts. I may even know a few more than you do. Enough at any rate for me to draw my own conclusions.

Some facts, though, are anything but incontrovertible, I say softly. Look at you, you traded in your German father for a Jewish one.

He nods. You're right, of course. The thing is, you can divide facts into two sorts. Father is dead, that's a fact. An incontrovertible fact. But the other fact, the fact that I had a German father when I was a boy, was eventually controverted by the appearance of another man with, let's say, better credentials. Facts of long standing can be superseded by others with a higher degree of credibility.

Didn't you ever have any doubts, I ask him, about Father really being your father? I mean, we never had 100 per cent certainty.

It would have driven me crazy to have doubts about that, he bursts out. Doubt and guilt are poisonous. You thought I looked just like him, you all did. I could see the likeness myself, even Father could see it. Wasn't that sufficient proof? I thought it was. I made up my mind it was sufficient.

A conscious decision, I say.

He smiles at me, but there is a glimmer of anxiety in his

eyes. Or have I got it all wrong? Is it just a projection of my own inability to be totally convinced about anything?

We sit close together, with him stroking my cheek and me taking hold of the hand stroking my cheek. It just depends on what you're after, he whispers. Most people don't want to change, they're attached to their feelings of remorse, indignation, to their bottled-up rage, their insecurity. They're terrified of what might happen if they ever let go of those feelings. That they might be replaced by something far worse.

Like my father, I say.

Like Father, he agrees.

To the Jewish cemetery please, Stefan says, in English. The cab driver has Tartar features. As if he's galloping across the *puzsta* on horseback he races the car out of the old city centre and into a neighbourhood that is never mentioned in the guide books. A sharp turn makes us fall against each other. The car swerves on to a dusty road running parallel to an old, gloomy railway track, the kind of thing you'd expect to see in a painting by Kiefer. Cemetery closed, he says, other time American go to Jewish cemetery, closed, today closed. Today it is not closed, Stefan insists, today there's a funeral. The driver shrugs his shoulders and sighs. He stops the car, nods his head in the direction of the gate. We pay the fare and get out.

The gate is locked. My father's got plenty of time. Stefan yells is anyone here? in every language under the sun. A young woman turns up with a bunch of keys. We enquire where the mortuary chapel is, to which she responds with a smile. She waves her arm over the cemetery expansively, as though bestowing a gift on us. We wander down a random alley. But you can hardly call this a cemetery! This is a battlefield of broken and sagging gravestones, tumble-down columns, obelisks. The sad city of the dead has been decked out with ivy and wild hop, with bushes and saplings trailing red-leaved virginia creeper. We quicken our pace, glance around nervously. Have patience, we're almost there. Only the graves bordering the chestnut-lined walks have been cleared of vegetation. Scraped clean. A swan carved in stone dies forever on the grave of Fleissig Sándor, 1869–1939. His death came just in time. In the neighbouring grave lie Eiseler Samuel and Böhm Klara. Beside them is a tombstone with an inscription in Hebrew and columns topped by a curved pediment decorated with an olive branch.

Are you coming, Stefan calls. We hurry down one lane after another, past overgrown sections where details of tombs light up in the sunbeams penetrating the leaf cover. Spitzer Mór, Klein Pinkas, Rózsavölgyi Katinka. That's my name! There it is, on a black marble obelisk! As if it's me lying there since time immemorial, and the agitated visitor observing my grave a stranger from an abstract future. My name! I shout to Stefan, to reassure myself that I am actually there. But he is twenty paces ahead of me and will not be distracted. The facts, stick to the facts. The only fact we must face today is that we are going to bury our father.

The ground is scattered with fallen chestnuts and yellow leaves, a lizard scuttles away, branches sway overhead. Every flutter is a reminder of death. They were born in the triangle between Dohány, Kertesz and Király utca, betrothed in Café Herzl, given in marriage in the Tabak temple, and now they lie here, in the stranglehold of tree roots. Don't they have any relatives, in America for instance, who could pay for the upkeep of their graves? The air in the cemetery is thick with outrage at the shameful neglect. Is this where we are to bury him, is this his dying wish?

Way ahead I see Stefan turning a corner. He beckons me to hurry up. My perception undergoes a subtle shift. Through my anguish I am seized with a sense of tragic beauty, a beauty that transcends the private fate of those who lie here. Amid the fallen obelisks, cracked slabs with Hebrew texts, ivied stone menoras and dying swans, Nature and Culture conspire to give the place the enchantment of the ruins of ancient Troy. How bleak by comparison is the strict uniformity of modern cemeteries in my country, where death has been purged of weeds for ever. Suddenly I hear the voice of my father breaking his customary silence to offer a wry opinion on his adopted country: as in life, so in death, the Dutch seem to think – they like their houses and their graves in straight rows.

Stefan runs back to me. We've made a mistake, he says panting, this cemetery's no longer in use. He unfolds the city plan he carries with him at all times, even today, in the inside pocket of his good suit. Look, he points, this is where we are now, at the far end of the Kerepesi temető. You can tell by that railway line we drove along. We are supposed to be all the way there – his finger swoops east-ward – at the Új Köztemetó.

But that's miles away, I protest.

Exactly, he says, so we had better get a move on.

Surely we're not going to be late for his funeral? It's unthinkable. Ever elusive when he was alive, is he going to escape us again now that he is to be buried? This is get-ting to be like a bad farce with the wrong people in the lead roles. Taxi, taxi, we plead with the young woman by the gate. Teleki László tér, she says, indicating the route we should take. Again that amused smile, which I can understand now. We run back along the road with the old railway track until it comes to an abrupt end. I hate it when railway tracks stop suddenly like that.

It flashes across my mind that the rabbi mentioned Teleki László tér when he was telling us about his grand-father who came from Tarnopol in Galicia, and who sold buttons and sewing necessities on the market. He said it was cut through by a diagonal tramline, which divided the grounds in two, a flea market on one side and a vegetable market on the other. That there used to be a small synagogue at number 22, that they were as poor as church mice and that they lived in Luiza Gasse. A Polish neighbourhood it was, he remembered it well. We steered him gently away from his musings, for we needed more practical information.

There is still a market there today, on one side of the track. The other side has been turned into a small park where men stand around looking bored. We go past a skip filled to overflowing and with more rubbish dumped all round. Plastic bags are blowing in the wind. A pair of tights dangles from the branch of a tree, underneath which stands an unattended baby carriage of a model I have only seen in old photographs. A man sinks his bare arm into a refuse bin, draws something out, sniffs it and puts it in his mouth. No trace of a synagogue as far as I can see, just dilapidated buildings. This is where the poorest wretches used to live. They still do, by the look of it. We make for the line of ramshackle taxis waiting at the corner of the park and climb into one, out of breath.

We won't be long now, we're hurtling across town in a rusty taxi from Teleki László tér to be with you as soon as we can. For all my efforts to get the feel of the city where my father and grandmother were born, to make it mine, I find I am a total stranger in these parts. I have allowed myself to be deceived by the beauty of the old town and the patina of history. From the windows of the taxi we see flashes of industrial sites, high-tension wires, rail tracks and dingy tower blocks from the days of Communism in a relentless staccato, cutting me off from the world I have been trying so hard to reconstruct. Nothing seems real. I catch a glimpse of something that is worse than bereavement. It is the underside of the world, where the sun never reaches. The poor soul who strays into his nether-world is doomed to live in the shadows for ever. There is no shelter, the cold spares no one in this desolate place where utter indifference reigns.

I can sense that Stefan is looking at me from the corner of his eye. He squeezes my hand. The sense of desolation, more frightening than all the rest, lifts again. We pass a sign pointing to the Roman Catholic section of the cemetery, where stonemasons line both sides of the road like sentries at the pearly gates. There are unhewn blocks of stone and finished slabs in all shapes and sizes, flower stalls spilling bouquets and wreaths, an assortment of gifts to accompany the dear departed on their final journey along with best wishes for an afterlife that will be better, more beautiful, than life on earth. There are lots of people milling around, could it be All Souls Day? I know practically nothing about Christian holidays, nor Jewish feast days for that matter. I have no idea what moves people to observe them. I cannot understand why my father turned to religion at the end of his life.

Stop, I tell the cab driver. Flowers! We must buy some flowers. I don't think they have flowers at Jewish funerals, Stefan says. Nonsense, I say, we must have flowers. I make a dash for the stalls massed with roses and chrysanthemums, chrysanthemums and roses. Not my favourite flowers. I choose some tea roses and large blooms flushed with pale orange.

I've been split apart into different selves, and it's the self that has no feeling that is preparing to bury her father in Budapest. She buys up all the yellow and orange roses in sight and asks for them to be arranged in a bouquet. She gives an approving nod to the flowerseller's offer of a ribbon to tie round the stalks.

They step into a white oriental-style building. It has three doors in the front, over which are three arched windows, each with a star of David in leaded glass. The dimly lit interior is furnished with rows of shiny black benches. On a raised platform at one end rests a coffin draped in black cloth. There is black everywhere, it's a statement of finality, of proof beyond all doubt. The rabbi is present, as well as a few members of the Jewish community centre who will act as pall bearers. A pair of distant cousins with whom he had been in contact in recent years are also there; they're the relatives who have dealt with the formalities surrounding the funeral. They speak only Hungarian.

There is nothing for it but to sit back in weary amazement for the duration of the rituals in a language she does not know. She is losing her father to Hungary, to age-old Jewish traditions. She is delivering him to their care, just as he delivered himself to what he came to believe were his rightful origins. The prayer intoned by the rabbi sounds like an arcane exorcism from another era, the vibrant symbol of what the mind cannot grasp. A melody of mourning, but also of hope. May the dead rise again.

She is not there when the coffin is carried outside, towards the Jewish section of the Új Köztemető. Nonetheless, she observes the scene in painfully sharp detail. More of the graves here have been cleared of creepers and weeds, it's true, but the impression of a battle-ground after the dust has settled is as strong as in the cemetery across town. The gravestones standing upright are like soldiers who have lost the power of speech, others have subsided against their neighbour or lie broken on the ground. The small cortège moves slowly along an avenue lined with dark, twisted trees, autumn leaves crackle underfoot. Arriving at a plot with fresh graves, it comes to a halt. The moment of standstill is full of portent. There is no going back. Closure is at hand. This part of the ritual is something she would rather not witness.

She does not look at the fresh earth, the spades, the men in black busying themselves like so many gardeners. She is not listening. Her eye is caught by the gravel lying on the next grave, a tidy arrangement of good wishes ready to escort the dead. Her eyes turn to her own surname engraved in gold on black marble. Elza. Yacov. The inscription underneath reads *Er wollte immer nur das beste.* Nothing but the best, indeed. In her head she can see Yacov facing right with a faraway look in his eyes. Something Uncle Miksa once said flashes across her mind. That his grandparents spoke German in the presence of their servants.

When no one is looking she gathers some gravel from the next grave and drops the little pebbles on the earth covering her father's coffin. A yellow chestnut leaf flutters down, comes to rest at the foot of the coffin. At the foot? Yes, where you would expect his feet to be resting.

We order a meal to be served in my room. I don't feel up to dining in the restaurant surrounded by all those hotel guests who have no idea I buried my father today. You're tired, Stefan says, pouring me a glass of wine. Here, take a sip, let's drink to us, to the living. The Tokay acts on me like a painkiller and a sedative at the same time, it immerses me in a sweet blur, an illusion of peaceful acceptance with sweet notes of never more and for ever. Tokay is an elixir of life.

We really shouldn't be doing this, I say, drinking all this wine on the day of the funeral. It's not disrespectful, Stefan says, it's a traditional custom. Getting high after a funeral is common to all cultures. The grief will come later, of its own accord, have no fear. Tomorrow, or the day after. Let's drink while we can enjoy it, for our days too are numbered. *Egészségére!* I call room service for another bottle.

What does *egészségére* mean, I ask warily. Cheers, he says.

My thoughts drift to his extraordinary good humour, which contrasts so shrilly with my father's unrelenting morosity. His level-headedness, his unflagging pursuit of rational solutions, his wish to make everyone happy. Over the years I have observed him from a distance, and some-times at close quarters, too. As long as I have known him he has been making two women happy at the same time. He's persuasive, talks them round, holds the problem of jealousy up to the light. His ever-rational explanation is that jealousy is irrelevant. This fits in with the ethos of the age, which dismisses such emotional ties as too restrictive. I'm deeply grateful that I am neither of these women, yet I would have given anything to be either of these women. He wanders in and out of their lives without guile, he picks flowers, distributes bouquets, his charm is infuriating. Their protestations drown in his eloquence, his intelligence. He's got a brain of steel, you might as well kick against a block of granite. As a scientist he sides against the prevailing trend in nuclear power, the cleanest of all sources of energy. He writes articles for newspapers and learned journals, loses idealistic friends, makes new ones. He is a friend to my father. With him my father is accepting in a way he never is with me.

I'm going to lie down for a bit, Stefan says. He rises from his chair, glass in hand, and stretches out on the bed.

Come, he motions with a wave of his arm.

There's a sense of repetition as I lie down on the bed beside him. A recollection of a tableau vivant, retrieved from long ago, dusted off and given a polish with an anti-static cloth. The headiness brought on by the Tokay intensifies the remembered image, making it so real that it melds imperceptibly with the present. He and I again, we're still the same, it's only the world that has changed. Hold me, I say, I've just buried my father. So have I, he says.

All that's missing now is a picture of heaven, he says, gazing up at the ceiling. The sky was only a pretext, I reply. He nods. There was no other way, he admits, we were just babes in the wood. He twists his head round to face me, our eyes meet. The moment when we first looked into each other's eyes, when we first saw each other and knew without knowing, that troubling moment comes rushing back to settle itself in a room at the Astoria Hotel. The sameness is inescapable, the way we were then is the way we are now. The desire is the same, too, and so is the scenario according to which it is inadmissible.

We're not babes in the wood any more, he whispers. He looks much more like my father now than when I first met him as a student. Yes, we've grown up since then, I say. He traces his finger along my cheek, yet another cheek among all those others his finger has traced. He puts his face close to mine, touches my throat with his lips. The Tokay has driven the blood to the surface of my body, just under the skin, magnifying each touch a thousand times. Time flies backwards, flowers crumple up into buds, raindrops rise up from the earth to form clouds, the water in the Danube flows upstream to the Black Forest, the dead rise again and walk backwards into their homes, we're like salmon returning to the stream where they hatched for a final fling before they die.

I break away from him. No, I stammer, only a few hours ago we were at the Új Köztemetó, you're the uncle of my children, your wife is my sister-in-law, your children and mine are cousins.

Oh Kata, he sighs, what can any of that possibly mean under the sun, the moon, under stars and planets? He waves his arm grandly at the ceiling, as if to say here they are in this very hotel room looking down at us from on high, and they're all yours. It is the generosity of his gesture, the way he offers the firmament to his love as his personal gift, that epitomizes the charm and seductiveness which they all found irresistible. Things have the meanings you assign to them.

That would be fine if we were as free as a bird, I protest, if we had no ties binding us to anyone or anything. As for me, I am tied, I am earth-bound, I can't take off and fly. I take other people's feelings into consideration.

Even when they're dead? he asks.

Yes, even when they're dead and buried.

He eyes me narrowly, then smiles as if I have reminded him of something. There's a faint air of helplessness about him – another tried and tested, irresistible part of his charm. Do you really believe, he grins, that you can actually stop wanting something simply by deciding you don't want it?

Oh please, I beg him, let's not get all philosophical again.

Your reasons for wanting certain things and not others are imposed by considerations of decency and compassion, he continues, undeterred. How typically feminine. He clasps my hands. Personal growth and development don't come into it at all, he says, it's sheer self-effacement.

Ah, how could I forget, I exclaim. We're condemned to freedom! We must employ our innate creativity to create ourselves, out of nothing, in a continual process of re-creation. Doing that involves taking conscious decisions, time after time. If you aren't prepared to let go of old, familiar certainties, out of fear or lethargy, you'll sink into oblivion and nothingness. But no one reads Sartre any more these days, do they? All that's left standing is the idea of wanting to be in control of our lives, the American way.

I have always loved you, he whispers.

Why are my defences crumbling? I can see right through his clever arguments, I know all about his tactics of persuasion, and yet.

I stammer that love may not be the right word, but that my life has been incomplete without him. It's as if I have missed my destiny, every experience I have had has been edged with incompleteness.

Come here. He gives me a commanding look. It's what I want, and it's what you want. He draws me close. My chin rests on his shoulder, his chin on mine. The closeness of our bodies while we face in opposite directions is achingly symbolic. I can feel a stirring of the old resentment – the things I wanted always came either too early in my life or too late. The young man who rolled off me and shook his fist in the air, cursing, is still there, looming in my thoughts. The image is so powerful, so conclusive that it dominates everything else, you can't undo what's done, surely he can see that. It is an image of total rejection. But there was a perfectly good reason for that. There's always some good reason.

He begins to kiss me, wildly and urgently. His fingers fumbling with the buttons of my black blouse arouse a sense of danger in me. My muscles stiffen, my entire body becomes tense, he is my worst enemy and never, ever will I lay down arms. No, I cry. I push him away, jump up from the bed. Go away, I say dully, turning to the window with my back to him. Please go away.

Kata, he moans, you don't mean that.

Go away, I repeat. I don't look at him. My turned back

is the only protection I've got, and I have no intention
of giving it up. Outside, in the wet asphalt of this city
which will always elude me, I notice the wavering reflection of street lamps and the headlights of passing cars. My
whole life has been nothing but the reflection of what
others have thought, done and felt in my name. A
conscious decision? What is that? Other than arrogance,
I mean.

Over the sound of my breathing I can hear him cross to
the door and leave the room. Now he is angry, too. I stare
out of the window, I am lost for ever. How like me to do
the wrong thing at the wrong time all over again. Tonight,
the night after the funeral, I manoeuvred myself into a situation where there was no room for grief in any real
sense. Instead I got myself entangled in an embarrassing
battle of wills, and I'm feeling lonelier than ever. He's
flying home tomorrow. I will be staying on for a few days
to tie up loose ends. I'll be meeting the cousins we saw at
the funeral, there will be someone from the Jewish community centre with us to act as interpreter. These things
would have been better dealt with by him, of course,
since he is the son. His readiness to leave these filial
duties to me, added to his attempt just now to seduce me
on the very day of the funeral, suddenly make him less
convincing as a son, the only son.

It has never occurred to me, I have never dared think it.
Nor do I dare think about what the German officer might
have looked like. The possibility that the blonde woman
with the curly hair might simply have had a predilection
for men of a certain appearance has never arisen. That

Stefan – apart from his looks and his love of music – doesn't resemble my father in any way doesn't prove that I've been mistaken for the past thirty years. If I have been mistaken the possibilities are endless, and they don't bear thinking about. I slam the door in their face, leave them out in the cold, all those projections of my own frustrated imagination, my own fear of intimacy with him, especially with him. Latecomers will not be admitted.

Tomorrow he will be gone for ever, the occasion will never arise again. I will return to the man with whom I have shared my life for the past twenty-five years. Such are the facts, the very facts Stefan holds in such high esteem. The realization that I have allowed the last opportunity to slip by will never go away. When I am old and delivered to the feebleness of my body, I will beat my forehead in anguish.

I think of him, in his room on the other side of the wall. I see myself through his eyes, and I go cold. Suddenly I am terrifyingly unassailable. I am like the girl in Fuseli's painting, all innocence pretending to be fast asleep while the devil preys on her. It would have been braver to wake up and look him straight in the eye. Stick out my tongue. I'd like myself the better for it. If only I'd had the strength to do that. Not strength, he whispers inside my head, a conscious decision.

I raise the bottle of Tokay to my lips and drink the last of the wine. I walk to the mirror. We regard one another, she and I. Black blouse open, pale skin freckled, hair mussed. I want you just the way you are, with straggly plaits and garlic necklace. A watercolour painting, the sublimated desire of someone long since dead. There's a quiet sort of encouragement in her eyes. Go on then, I haven't got for ever. I could weep over her, over me. My mascara would run, and then, streaked with war paint, I would dare at last. Go on, do it. She is directing me to the door. Really? She nods. Life is for the living. Treading carefully I open the door and shut it behind me. Never before have two metres of dun-coloured carpet struck me as offering endless possibilities. For one thing, I could walk right past that door, down the corridor, into the lift, out of the hotel, have nothing to blame myself for. Wanting something you don't want, he jeers.

My knuckles rap timidly on the wood. It almost feels like school, like having to present yourself to the head teacher after being sent out of the classroom. He answers the door. I'm taken aback by the grave expression on his face, which makes him look old. I am Kata Rózsavölgyi, I say, my father will play you a czardas on his cello if you ask him. He draws me into the room, using his other hand to push the door shut behind me. Shshshs, he motions, not a word. Come. Come.

Come. Come. A house in a quiet little street. Upstairs in that little house lives my dear sweet Reyzele. Mmmmm. Wait my love, wait, I'll be ready in a minute. Take another little turn. One, two, three! Mmmmm. At the foot of the stairs I take her in my arms, kiss her softly on the top of her head. Come! Come! Come!

Uncle Miksa has launched into song, eliciting a sigh of resignation from my father. Does he think it's a silly song, or does it bring back memories he would rather not contemplate? But he translates the Yiddish for me anyway, so that I can sing along with him in my own language.

We hold each other tight as if we have just escaped death by drowning, as if our bodies have been cast up on the shore by a wave. All those moments in all those years when our eyes met while we pretended not to know what we saw, or pretended it was anything but what we saw, no matter what – all those past moments fuse with the present. A dragonfly feathering the water, taking flight, it is nothing, soon forgotten. It is there, it is all there is. All those moments running into one, passing through depths and heights and more rarefied regions on their way here, to earth, where bliss becomes unbearable and we are washed ashore as the flotsam of lust.

Our bodies have slid apart. He caresses me pensively, his fingers follow the contours of my body. My body comes alive under his hands, it is reborn, it glistens with newness, ˙eagerly gulps the air that everyone breathes. There's not a trace of nervous tension, no need to prove anything at all. I stroke him. For the past thirty years my fingertips have tingled with pent-up longing for the touch of his skin, and at last they are free to roam where they please. They take possession avidly, claiming him as their own, never to be abandoned. After he has gone, the touch of his skin, his hair, will be etched into my fingertips, my mouth for ever.

Then everything starts all over again, it is bewildering and at the same time somehow melancholy, for the moment has not only been so long in coming but may also never come again. His body is as familiar to me as my own, and yet it has been untouchable, and will be so once more. Our union carries within it the doom of parting, and in the half-light of imminent separation sensual pleasures run deliciously, unendurably deep. It is never the body that is to blame.

I've missed my sky, Stefan says. Every house I have lived in, every bedroom I've had since then, has reminded me of what I was missing. Heaven.

I'll paint you a new one, I propose jokingly. Thinking of his bedroom, his women, I tell him I couldn't stand a man being unfaithful to me.

That's all right then, he grins, looking at me with glittery eyes, because you're the one I'm being unfaithful with, not to. By being unfaithful with you I'm faithful to myself. To us. He buries his nose in my hair. Sometimes, he says, I'd see your hair streaking across my dreams. To remind me that you were still there lurking deep inside me, like an unkept promise.

Talk about being unfaithful, he goes on, tensing the muscles of his jaw, I never told you the worst part. About the two of them.

Are you sure this is the right time, I say in a plaintive voice. I want the purring contentment that has come over us to last for ever.

This is the perfect time, he maintains, it concerns both of us, you as well as me, whether we like it or not. He draws me close. My cheek against his chest, while he talks I can feel the vibration of his vocal chords. I can feel that he is alive, that I am alive, that the entire universe is alive through us.

As I listen to his voice, which is calm now as if he were speaking of trivial everyday matters, the room in the Astoria Hotel dissolves. This blessed room, the hotel, the city, they evaporate in my consciousness. Time shrinks and shrivels into a cramped overcrowded elevator where there's not enough oxygen to go round.

Remember I told you about the hole in the wooden partition between her bedroom and the alcove he used as his hideout? Did you ever stop to think about the significance of that little knot in the wood that had fallen out? No, I say under my breath. Saying no like that gives me a presentiment of what is to come. I have never thought about it, I have never dared to.

She could have received her lover in the living room, he says, that would have been more private, and besides, there was a divan there for visiting relatives who stayed the night. But no, she chose to receive him in her bedroom, so that he could watch them through the little hole. So that the man she loved would . . . You can't call that love, I blurt. Yes, it was love. She wanted the man she loved in her own special way to see what went on in the bedroom, in the very bed that she shared with him at night.

She actually wanted to make him suffer? I gasp, my throat tightens. She took pleasure in his misery?

Yes, and his jealousy was even greater than his fear. He writhed in agony, there in that alcove, he tore his hair out. If he'd been a voyeur he might have had a different experience, but he wasn't, so he suffered. He could see the cap with the emblem hanging on the bedpost, the uniform lying on the chair, the naked buttocks of the man who would have reported him at once had he suspected his presence on the other side of the partition. And she enjoyed every minute. She did all the things with the other man that she refused to do with him. As if they were actors in a film made up exclusively of scenes that would not have made it past the censors in those days.

A blanket, I say, sitting up. Let me get the blanket, I'm cold.

Once the man had gone, wearing his cap and uniform she would want her secret lodger. He was the icing on the cake. His jealousy and terror aroused her.

And Father? . . . I hardly dare ask.

He did what she wanted him to do. She forced him, she had power over him. Vagina dentata, he grins, that's where I'm coming from.

We lie side by side, each of us locked up in the inability to put this in any perspective, to make little of it. Now and then a car rumbles in the distance. In the desolation of a world inhabited by men I glimpse my father, before he became my father. His sole possession in the world is his cello. He is in a foreign country, he doesn't speak the language. There is a war on. She has everything she could wish for, including power. She takes pleasure in undermining the morale, the vitality, the self-respect of the man who is not yet my father. She is intent on emerging victorious from her double orgies at his expense. It was never enough, she always wanted more. There is a scientific name for her condition. You will come across it in medical handbooks, famous case histories, pornographic magazines. But there are no words to describe it.

I clear my throat. When did he tell you this?

It was quite soon after we met. He said: I'll be honest with you. Perhaps something will come of it, of us being together as father and son, but first I'll tell you what it was like. You mustn't cherish impossible illusions. I am not the man I once was, long ago.

Did he tell you what it was like for him after the war, how he got over it? He didn't get over it. He should have been with his family, he said. Instead of being there for them he became a plaything for a perverse woman, and that's how he survived. The thing he found most humiliating of all, which made him shrink from himself in disgust, was that his body had gone on loving her. Like an invalid who can't live without his medicine, however terrible the side-effects. Shame is not an adequate description of what he felt, he said, nor is guilt. If there had been a word for something worse than shame and guilt combined, he would have used it. He would have stood in some lonely place where no one could hear and he would have screamed that word over and over again, a thousand times, until its sharp edges gradually wore down so there would, perhaps, only be a nudge of pain left. He thought there might be such a word, a truly liberating word, but he didn't know what it was.

So he preferred to keep silent, I say, and all that time we thought it was our fault, that we were doing something wrong, that we weren't good enough the way we were.

The presence of his warm body beside me is soothing, reassuring in a brotherly way. We listen together to the silence. The stillness of night-time Budapest reverberates with the echoes of those who once lived there. You can hear them in the rush of the Danube, in the ripples of the water that has no conscience, you can hear them in the gurgle of a subterranean spring, in the bubbles that rise to the surface and pop. A vague echo of past and future hangs over the roofs, you can never say that quiet reigns in a city such as this, that people have stopped oppressing other people, that their horror of the never-ending violence has taught them to cast it out of their private microcosm. A feeling of futility comes over me when I think of the relentless urge people have to define themselves at the expense of others, their compulsion to give orders, to dominate men, animals, things.

But you, I say softly, you seem to like having two lovers on the go at the same time, too.

That's different! He sits bolt upright, fuming. How stupid of me! What on earth can have made me say a thing like that! He never forced anyone to do anything. The women he has had relationships with were free to come and go as they pleased, it was their choice. That's completely different. How dare I equate that with his mother's ruthless abuse of power!

I'm not equating the two, I say. I'm sorry. He calms down, stretches out on the bed again. I ask him if he ever

confronted his mother with what his father told him. He
certainly did. He went to see her the very same day. She
drove him wild with her denials, none of it was true, all
she had wanted was to save his life, because she loved
him. She had taken up with a German out of love for him.
Not that he ever showed any gratitude, he never said a
word of thanks. The man she had protected left her in the
lurch, a single mother amid hostile neighbours. If only he
had come forward, just a brief statement to the neighbours would have been enough to save her and her child
a lot of misery. But he made a run for it, at the first opportunity. The man who had been her greatest love, still was
in fact, just sneaked off. She had no intention of defending herself against the accusations of her son, he didn't
know what he was talking about, how could he judge?

It's incredible, I say, how resourceful people are in
distorting the truth. Just to ease their own conscience.

I'm not so sure she has a conscience, says Stefan.

I left her on her own, wallowing in self-pity. For years
we didn't see each other at all. For all that time his
mother didn't enter his mind. He didn't miss her, his
dislike of her was so intense that he banished her from his
thoughts. Nor could he bear to think of himself as a boy
with his mother. Because she had adored him, no one
could deny that, and she had spoilt him. She had indulged
him when he was young, for she would not have him feel
deprived in any way. Did he like music? He had his own
gramophone, as well as a collection of records, long
before any of his classmates. In the Fifties that was, when
money was tight. Was he interested in science? She

bought him books, a series for children devoted to Einstein, Edison, Madame Curie. She gave him a science kit for him to do experiments with, she was his audience when he made things explode or vanish. No, he did not think of her at all for years.

What about now? I ask.

Well, he sighs, now she's old and forgetful. She's depressed, can't stand the dereliction of her body. She doesn't remember the accusations he made. He goes to visit her now and then, she has forgotten all those years when they were not on speaking terms. He feels an abstract sort of compassion for her, she is his mother.

My fingertips stroke his Adam's apple. I am moved by his Adam's apple. Emotions can so constrict this delicate organ as to prevent it from making a sound. Even now it is not so much his voice that I hear but the silence of my father, the distinctly audible absence of any reassuring sound.

I'm going to sleep, Stefan says, I've got to get up early tomorrow. I love you, for ever.

He kisses me. I can feel his body relax, I can hear his regular breathing. In this release of tension, in the regularity of his breathing, he is already escaping me. We will part, I am to be left behind. He is strong. He has learned how to turn a switch in his head and fall asleep whatever the circumstances.

The girl I have been searching for is wandering in a vast, empty plain, brilliantly lit. She is wearing her sandy-coloured high-necked dress, more like a pinafore than a dress. It's as if I'm looking at her in the tremulous light of a television screen. As she comes closer she grows older. From being the girl in the watercolour she turns into the mother in the photographs. She beckons me. Come. Come. She spreads her arms.

She's not my grandmother, it's me. I stretch out my arms. I walk towards myself, but the other me draws back, then to one side, until she finally slides off the screen. She who is not my grandmother but myself draws back before my very eyes and moves sideways out of the frame, over the edge. Suddenly she is gone, and I am left empty-handed on an empty, blinding plain.

I wake up with a start. The first thing I do is reach out to touch him, expecting not to find him there. But he is. Waking up in the middle of the night and finding him at her side! For her it is perfectly normal, and will remain so. It is tempting to see life as an evolving story-line in which striving, hoping and waiting will ultimately be rewarded. If this night has been my reward, do I still want to hear the rest?

Keeping very still, I listen to him breathe. As I lie there, listening, I can already feel the longing for this night that will haunt me for the rest of my life.